THE SHOWDOWN

Also by Jessica Burkhart

THE SADDLEHILL ACADEMY SERIES
Sweet & Bitter Rivals

THE CANTERWOOD CREST SERIES

For older readers
Life Inside My Mind

For younger readers
THE UNICORN MAGIC SERIES

Saddlehill Academy

THE SHOWDOWN

JESSICA BURKHART

Aladdin

New York   London   Toronto   Sydney   New Delhi

ALADDIN
An imprint of Simon & Schuster Children's Publishing Division
1230 Avenue of the Americas, New York, New York 10020
First Aladdin hardcover edition July 2023
Text copyright © 2023 by Jessica Burkhart
Jacket illustration copyright © 2023 by Lana Dudarenko
Jacket filigree and crest by ProVectors/iStock
Jacket horses by SvetlanaSoloveva/iStock
Also available in an Aladdin paperback edition.
All rights reserved, including the right of reproduction in whole or in part in any form.
ALADDIN and related logo are registered trademarks of Simon & Schuster, Inc.
For information about special discounts for bulk purchases, please contact
Simon & Schuster Special Sales at 1-866-506-1949 or business@simonandschuster.com.
The Simon & Schuster Speakers Bureau can bring authors to your live event.
For more information or to book an event contact the Simon & Schuster Speakers Bureau
at 1-866-248-3049 or visit our website at www.simonspeakers.com.
Jacket designed by Karin Paprocki
Interior designed by Mike Rosamilia
The text of this book was set in Adobe Garamond Pro.
Manufactured in the United States of America 0623 FFG
2 4 6 8 10 9 7 5 3 1
Library of Congress Cataloging-in-Publication Data
Names: Burkhart, Jessica, author.
Title: The showdown / by Jessica Burkhart.
Description: First Aladdin paperback edition. | New York : Aladdin, 2023. |
Series: Saddlehill Academy ; 2 | Audience: Ages 9–13. | Summary: Abby is worried her unmasked
blackmailer will expose the one secret she cannot risk getting out, and to make matters worse, the
drama is affecting her performance on Beau, putting her place on the team in jeopardy.
Identifiers: LCCN 2022053303 (print) | LCCN 2022053304 (ebook) |
ISBN 9781665912921 (pbk) | ISBN 9781665912938 (hc) | ISBN 9781665912945 (ebook)
Subjects: CYAC: Boarding schools—Fiction. | Schools—Fiction. | Horsemanship—Fiction. |
Secrets—Fiction. | Extortion—Fiction.
Classification: LCC PZ7.B92287 Sh 2023 (print) | LCC PZ7.B92287 (ebook) | DDC [Fic]—dc23
LC record available at https://lccn.loc.gov/2022053303
LC ebook record available at https://lccn.loc.gov/2022053304

This one's for Aly Heller and Jessi Smith,
my wonderful editors, who are
helping me rebuild

How Could She?

I DIDN'T EVEN PAY ATTENTION TO WHERE I ran. As fast as I could, I bolted down the lane, away from Emery Flynn. I couldn't stand being around her for another second, not after what she'd done. Not after she'd protected my classmate and fellow rider, Nina aka the Truth X. Poser. The person who had filmed me without my consent, doctored the video, and leaked it to make it sound as if I hated Emery. My own stepsister knew the truth, but she never spoke up. She just let Nina torment me.

Tears streamed down my cheeks as I skidded to a halt

near the hay barn at Foxbury. Riders from my stable and nearby barns packed the grounds, thanks to this weekend's three-day event. The main barn was the last place I wanted to be right now, even though I wished I could have run to Beau, my horse.

Instead, I darted into the hay barn and scrambled up one of the ladders to the hayloft. I threw myself down behind a tall stack of hay bales and tried to breathe.

How could Emery do this to me? I'd poured my heart out to her and let her in, telling her all the ways the TXP had hurt me and had made me distrust everyone around me except for my closest friends. Except for Emery. I hadn't thought I'd needed to worry about her.

I wiped my cheeks with the back of my hand, thinking the tears had finally slowed. But a fresh wave of hurt and anger washed over me, and I kept crying.

Every conversation between Emery and me since I'd been back at Saddlehill Academy came back to me.

Every text.

Every talk.

Everything.

Why had she done it? Emery could have picked anyone

else in Charles House, where she lived with Nina, to befriend. It didn't have to be Nina, who'd gone from chill and fun to mean and snarky after she'd become tight with Selly Hollis.

And when Emery had found out how Nina had been the one trying to wreck my life, she should have come to me. Period. There were no excuses. After the talks we'd had about how we were trying to become friends so this whole new-stepsisters thing wouldn't be so awkward and hard, she'd done that.

I wasn't going to speak to her ever again.

Ever. Again.

Had she ever really even liked me? Or had she wanted to be Nina's friend all along and she was just pretending with me to get info to share with Nina?

Below me, boots tapped down the aisle. I held my breath, sure it was Emery wanting to try and talk to me and apologize. I didn't move, and I stayed with my arms curled around my legs even when I heard someone coming up the ladder to the hayloft.

"Abby?"

It wasn't Emery after all.

"Over here," I croaked.

Thea Song, one of my two best friends, popped into view as she peered around a stack of hay bales, spotting me.

I burst into a fresh round of tears just seeing a friendly face. Thea was on the loft floor next to me in seconds, wrapping her arms around me.

"I don't know what happened," she said, "but Emery came up to me, super upset, and said I should check on you. One of the Lennox Hill riders said she'd seen you run in here."

"Emery happened," I said. "She's known who the TXP is!"

Thea sat back so she could see my face, her eyes wide. "She *what* now?"

"I got this weird text from the TXP, and it said Emery was hiding something. So I asked her about it. Totally all nonchalant, because I thought it was just the TXP trying to cause trouble and stir stuff up between us. But Emery . . . she started apologizing and telling me she didn't mean to hurt me, but she knew who the TXP was."

"You're joking!"

"Do I look like I'm joking?" I practically shrieked the question.

Thea winced. "Sorry. I'm in shock. I don't know what to say right now. Who is it? Who's the TXP?"

"Nina." I gritted my teeth. "It was Nina all along."

"No way! Are you sure?" Thea shook her head. "I can't believe this. Like, *Nina*?!"

"I mean, that's what Emery said, so yeah. I haven't talked to Nina yet, but you can bet I will."

"And she told Emery this?" Thea asked. "That she's the TXP, and she's been harassing you?"

"Yup. Sounds like she even bragged about it to Emery. And Emery's been covering for her."

"This is wild," Thea said.

"I know." I rubbed my forehead, feeling the anger start overtaking the hurt and sadness.

Tears welled up in my eyes, but I swallowed hard, trying not to cry. Emery was *so* not worth my tears.

"I really thought that you two were going to be okay," Thea said, her brown eyes on mine. "You did the right thing when the TXP video broke. You went straight to Emery and talked to her, even though it was scary and hard to have that convo." Thea sighed. "I know that wasn't easy."

Anger burned in my chest when I thought about that talk with Emery. I'd been so terrified that someone else's lie was going to ruin our new, budding friendship. Even though it was awkward with my dad marrying her mom, I'd promised myself I'd try. Not just for me, but for my dad. For all of us. But now? Things were a dumpster fire.

"I thought we were good after that too," I said. "For the rest of the week, she was totally fine toward me. But then, when she wanted to have that talk and told me, 'You don't have to keep looking for the TXP, Abby. I believe you, Abby,' she wasn't looking out for me. At *all*."

"She was looking out for herself."

"I'm so stupid."

Thea reached over, taking my hand. "No, you're not, Abs."

"I should have known! I was so wrapped up in trying to uncover the TXP's identity that I missed it."

"*Stop.* There was no way for you to have known Emery was involved. You didn't miss anything."

"I told Vivi not to put her on our suspect list!"

"Because she's your stepsister," Thea said. "Abby, I wouldn't have put her on my list either. You're a good person, so you just thought she'd be one too."

"If this is what happens when I'm a good person, forget it," I grumbled. "I'm done."

"Abby."

"I'm serious. I need to go back to school. I don't want to see Emery right now. Well, ever. But especially not right now."

Thea stood and stuck out a hand to me. "C'mon. The show's over today for our team, anyway. As captain, I'll text Rebecca and tell her we left."

Oops, right. Rebecca. I cringed a little, hoping word of my argument with Emery wouldn't reach my riding instructor.

I reached up, clasped Thea's hand in mine, and let her pull me to my feet.

"Let's get you back to school," Thea said.

Squad of Awful People

WHEN WE GOT BACK, THEA WALKED me to my dorm room in Amherst House and shut the door behind us. My phone buzzed in my hand, and I looked at the screen.

Four new texts from Emery.

I dismissed every notification without even opening them, put my phone on do not disturb, and laid it facedown on my desk.

"Where's Vivi?" Thea asked.

I sniffled, thinking of my other best friend and roommate,

as I sat down at the end of my bed. "She's probably doing something at the theater. I think she had a meeting with her acting class."

"Okay, well, how about this: Why don't you shower and get into comfy clothes, I'll do the same, and we can all hang later to talk?" Thea eyed me. "Or not—we don't have to talk. It's totally up to you."

"Talking is good," I mumbled.

"I won't be gone long, okay?" There was concern all over Thea's face, and I couldn't help but feel bad for hijacking the rest of her Friday.

I nodded, out of words, looking down at my lap. All I could do was stare blankly at my breeches as I rubbed my thumb over the fabric in mindless circles.

I couldn't believe Emery had lied to me about being with Nina on the day when the TXP had sneaked into my room and vandalized my whiteboard.

I faintly heard Thea go into my bathroom, flick on the light, and turn on the shower.

"C'mon, Abs," she said. She pulled me to my feet and pushed me into the bathroom. "Go shower. I'll be back soon!"

And then she was gone.

I stayed under the hot water for far too long, feeling numb. Everything had been looking up. But now? The new "family" that Natalie, Dad, Emery, and I had been trying to build was ruined.

After I tugged on clean leggings and an old T-shirt, I towel-dried my hair and flopped onto my bed. I lay there, staring at the ceiling, until Thea came back, with Vivi right behind her.

"I texted Vivi and told her everything," Thea explained, "and we ran into each other on the way in."

"Abby," Vivi said, coming over and hugging me. "I'm so sorry."

I squeezed her back, determined not to cry about this anymore. "How could she?" I asked. "I asked Thea that question, and it's all I keep asking myself. But how could Emery do that?"

I pulled myself off my bed, and the three of us sat on the yellow rug in front of the fireplace.

"Does she want to be part of that group?" Thea asked. "Nina and Selly?"

I shrugged. "I was too shocked by what she'd said to even ask her that. I definitely don't want to talk to her now to find out either. If she wants to be their bestie, she can have them. They all deserve each other."

"They so do," Thea said. "They can be their own squad of awful people. There, when I'm talking about them in the future, that's what I'm calling them. SOAP."

I snorted. "I like it. Emery and I are so done. Thank god she's not in any of my classes at school, so I won't have to see her face then. But *yay*. Every single riding lesson, she'll be there."

"I know you're still upset," Thea said, "and I would be too. But did you realize what this means?"

"What?"

"You know the Truth X. Poser's identity," Thea said, smiling a little. "This means you can go to Molly and tell her exactly what Nina did to you. Heck, once Rebecca finds out? She'll probably kick Nina off the team!"

Molly was the Amherst House resident advisor, or RA. My friends exchanged wide-eyed looks.

"Ahhh, that's right," Vivi said. "Abs, you should go talk to Molly now. I'll go with you, if you want."

"I will too," Thea said. "This is huge."

I swallowed, shaking my head, as panic started to sweep

over me. This was my chance to tell my best friends exactly what I'd done to Selly—how I'd accidentally cost her a shot at team captain and messed up the start of her show season last year—but I couldn't begin to form the words.

"I'm not ready right now," I said, my voice a little squeaky. "I need some time to process first."

"I understand," Thea said. "But why wait?"

Vivi nodded, looking from Thea to me. "You've been working so hard on figuring this out. Are you sure you don't want to go talk to Molly?"

You should tell them the truth, I yelled to myself. *Just do it! Tell them it was an accident, a mix-up, and I didn't mean to make Selly miss her class.* But somehow, Nina knew, and if I told anyone what she'd done to me, she'd tell Selly my secret. And Selly wasn't one to forgive and forget—she'd make my life miserable.

"I'm sure," I said, finally answering Vivi. "Like I said, time to process and figure out exactly what to do with this information."

"The thing to do is tell Molly," Thea said.

Vivi leaned forward, touching my arm. "I know you're scared."

You have no idea, I thought.

"But don't let Nina hold this over you any longer," Vivi continued. "She's done enough. If you're afraid to talk to someone because you're worried about retaliation, I get it. I do. But Thea and I will do everything we can to make sure she doesn't come after you again."

"I know," I said, "and thank you." I paused, trying not to outright lie to my friends. "I could run off and tell Molly right now, yeah, but I could also sit on it, think things over, and decide how to make Nina really sorry."

A corner of Thea's mouth quirked up in a grin. "I like that. It isn't a terrible idea."

"Maybe she expects you to rat her out immediately," Vivi said, "and this plan of making her wait and wonder what exactly you're going to do with this information could make her so worried."

"She deserves to be worried," I murmured. "After all of this, it's kind of the least she deserves."

"I couldn't agree more," Vivi said. She stretched her legs out in front of her as she traded a quick look with Thea.

"What?" I asked. "What was that look for?"

Another look between them, but they both smiled.

"You okay with me spending the night?" Thea asked. "Vivi's cool if I do."

"Of course!" I said. "I'd rather not be alone right now."

"Well, everything's a mess, but at least Emery's not on our show team," Thea said, "so that should help. But you know Rebecca. She's not going to want to see an ounce of tension between you two. Anywhere. She has a sixth sense about that stuff."

"You're right. I'm lucky Rebecca didn't see any of it today." I grimaced. "I tore down that lane so fast, and I wasn't paying attention at all. If she'd seen me running like that around the other competitors' horses, she would have flipped out."

"Yeaaaah," Thea said. "That would have been bad."

"I'll be careful during the show," I said. "Promise. I'll stay away from Emery and Nina. If Rebecca gathers us together to talk or something, I'll be cool. I can fake it."

Thea brushed her long black hair over one shoulder. "Then, the second you're off stable grounds, all bets are off."

That made me smile. "Exactly."

"Are you going to tell your dad?" Thea asked. "He was sooo 'how's it going with Emery?' that I bet he'll know something is up between you two."

"I don't know," I said. "I doubt I'll tell him. At least, not right now. He'd probably tell me to forgive her and get one of the teachers to stick us in a room together so we could talk and hug it out." I folded my arms across my chest. "I don't want that."

Vivi and Thea nodded.

Plus, I didn't have the kind of relationship with my dad where I went to him with friendship drama. Granted, this was a little bigger than a disagreement with a friend. But still. It would be weird for me to go to him about his other daughter and our issues. I wouldn't even know how to begin having that convo with Dad.

"Let's order dinner," Thea said. "And then we can eat and watch some Netflix."

"That sounds perfect," I said.

Thea busied herself ordering our Chinese food.

I settled back onto the oversized pillows we'd laid on the floor, trying to make myself as comfy as possible.

"Where do you think Emery is right now?" Thea asked.

I started to shrug, but then I remembered. "Her mom's in town. My dad was supposed to come too, but he needed an extra day. She was in the stands watching Emery compete.

So they're probably having a super-fun night out."

"I wish I knew if she was having a good time or if she was miserable," Vivi said. She shrugged one shoulder. "It's petty, but I hope her dinner was cold and way too salty."

"Vivi," Thea said, but she laughed.

"Has she texted you? Called?" Vivi asked.

"Oh, she's texted plenty," I said, "but I put my phone on silent." I stood and swiped it off the desk. "Do we want to know what she said or nah?"

"If you want to, I do," Thea said.

I thought for a few seconds, trying to decide. Then I sighed. "Let's see what she had to say." I tapped on Emery's messages. "Okay, she said, 'Abby, I'm so sorry. Please let me explain.' Then, 'I know you're upset, and I would be too. But can we talk, please?' Next message says, 'I wasn't trying to protect Nina. I didn't want any trouble with anyone.' Her last text says, 'Can we talk tomorrow?'"

"Huh," Thea said.

Vivi rolled her eyes. "That's really all she has to say?"

"So underwhelming," Thea said. "I thought you'd have a mountain of long texts. A novel-length apology of texts."

"And why doesn't she want to talk to you tonight?" Vivi

asked. "I dunno, if I did what she did? My schedule would be very, *very* open to talking to the other person."

"Mine, too," I said. "I guess she really is busy with her mom tonight. And I don't even want to talk to her, so whatever."

Vivi shook her head. "I'm so sorry, Abs. I don't know Emery at all, but still—this is wild. Based on everything you've told me about her, she didn't seem like the type of person to do this."

"I thought I was getting to know her," I said, "but I never saw this coming."

"Speaking of seeing things," Thea said. "How did we miss this with Nina? Seriously, we really messed up."

I immediately felt guilty. I hated seeing Thea feel bad about Nina when she'd never had all the facts. I wished I could find it in me to tell them about Selly, but I was just too scared. How could I tell my two best friends that I'd been keeping a big secret from them since last year?

"No, no, we didn't," I said. "It's on Emery—not on us. I only took Nina off the list because Emery said she was with her when the TXP broke into our room. It was a lie. She wasn't with Nina."

"Well, that's true," Vivi said. "But I kind of took her off my personal list before then. I didn't see it in Nina to do this, especially not after how you two were friendly last year. Emery sure made me look away from Nina too."

The more I thought about it all, the angrier I got. It felt like tiny flames of anger burned under my skin.

My screen lit up, catching my attention even though my phone was still on silent.

It was Dad!

I Quit

MY DAD'S CALLING," I SAID, SMILING
despite everything. He was coming tomorrow,
and even thinking about his upcoming visit
made me happy.

"Talk if you want," Thea said. "We'll go wait for the food."

"Okay, I won't be long," I said, answering the phone as my
friends slipped out the door. "Hi, Dad!"

I tried to keep any hint that something was wrong out
of my voice. I didn't want him to know about what had been
going on with Emery. Not yet, anyway.

"Hi, hon," Dad said. "How did today go?"

His familiar voice made a lump form in my throat. Even though he didn't know what was going on, hearing his voice helped.

"Dressage went really well," I said. "Beau and I had our best test to date. He was so good, and he did everything I asked. I'm so proud of him."

"Abs, that's fantastic!" Dad said. I could hear the smile in his voice. "I'm so proud of you. Beau too, of course, but you more. Every year, you keep growing as a rider."

I couldn't help but smile. I'd been in love with horses since I could walk and had started riding at my local stable on the lesson ponies. But two years ago, Dad gave me Beau so I could have a horse of my very own. It was love at first sight!

"Thanks, Dad." I felt my mood lift as we talked, and for a moment, I could almost pretend there were no hurt feelings, no anger, and no betrayal by Emery. "I can't wait for you to see us compete tomorrow. If it goes anything like today, it's going to be a *good* phase. What time do you think you'll get here?"

I started to babble a bit as the excitement of Dad coming to see me started to wash over me. I'd been so focused on showing today—and then the entire mess with Emery had happened—that I'd barely had any time to think about Dad coming tomorrow.

"Whatever time you get here, I'll work it out! Just text me. And then we can figure out what we want to do and where we want to go." The words spilled out. "We could grab food at—"

"Abby, about tomorrow," Dad interrupted.

"Daaad. Don't tell me you're going to be late. Or that you have to leave super ridiculously early the next morning. You were already supposed to come *today*."

"I hate doing this, sweetie, but I can't come for the show. I'm so sorry."

I stilled, then shook my head, sure I'd heard him wrong.

"What? You're not coming?"

"I want to be there," Dad continued. "You know I do."

"No," I spat out. "I actually don't know that at all."

"Abby, I just found out that I have to work and go into the office. It's not something I can miss."

"You told me you had time off." My voice rose with every word. "I've been waiting for this all week! And tomorrow's Saturday. Are you really selling insurance on a Saturday?"

"Honey, I know," Dad said. "Me too. I wouldn't miss this unless I had no choice."

Tears started falling again for the hundredth time that day. "You have a choice, Dad. You chose work. *Again.* Like always. Whenever it's me or work? You choose work."

"That's not true." Dad sounded hurt, but I didn't care. I was fresh out of caring right now.

"It is. Although I'm sure you'd be here for one person."

"That's not fair, Abby," Dad said. "I married Natalie, but that doesn't mean I've chosen her over you. I thought you were—"

"This isn't about Natalie! It's about *Emery*! God, Dad, you don't get it. At all!"

I didn't even know where it came from, but anger bubbled in my chest and spilled over.

"Abby," Dad said, a hint of warning in his tone. "I haven't done anything different for Emery than I've done for you."

That was part of the problem! Emery wasn't me. She wasn't his actual daughter. No matter what happened, Emery still had her mom. I didn't. My mom was long gone, and seeing Emery with hers made resentment burn in my chest.

"If you'd made plans with Emery, you would have kept them," I said, yelling again. I didn't care if I got in trouble later for screaming at him. This was all too big to keep inside.

It was too much on top of everything else that had happened today. "You would have shown up to be with your shiny new daughter. I knew this would happen! You never even had time for *one* daughter."

"Abigail."

Dad was super hurt.

But I was too angry to care. My eyes blurred with tears, and I swiped at them with my free hand. I didn't want to cry again. I was sick of crying.

"You say you're going to be there for me, but you aren't. And this isn't easy. I'm away at school. When you say you're going to show up? You show up. You're the company president, Dad. You make the rules. You could be here! But you aren't."

"I want to be there. I'm so sorry, Abby, that I'm making you feel like I don't. This is a big deal for me and for work. It's an important account that—"

"And I'm not important?" I interrupted.

"That's not what I said. I'm explaining to you the reason why I have to cancel."

I couldn't listen to him anymore. The excuses were doing nothing but make me more upset. I'd heard so many from him throughout my life. He was a great dad when he was around, and normally, I loved the attention from him. But at this moment, I didn't want it anymore. I wanted him to leave me alone.

"I have to go," I said. "Maybe next time, I'll make sure to include Emery in our plans so you actually show up. Bye, Dad."

Before he could say another word, I ended the call and turned my phone all the way off just as Thea and Vivi—with takeout and sodas in hand—let themselves into the room.

"What's wrong?" Vivi asked, eyeing me. "Did you tell your dad about Emery?"

I shook my head. "Nope! He called me to cancel. He's not coming tomorrow."

My friends plopped next to me, putting the food and drinks down.

"What? Why not?" Vivi asked, wide-eyed.

"He's 'working.'"

Thea rubbed her forehead. "I'm so sorry, Abs. That's so unfair."

Vivi opened the takeout bag, got her container of sesame chicken, and passed the egg-drop soup to Thea. She reached back in for my soup, but I shook my head.

"I'm going to pass for right now," I said. "I was starting to get hungry, but not anymore."

"We can wait and eat later with you," Thea said, putting down her food.

"No, eat," I said. "I want you to."

I stretched my legs out in front of me and lay on my back, staring up at the ceiling while my friends ate. The scent of Chinese food, which normally made me super hungry and reminded me of Friday nights last year when Vivi and I always ordered Chinese, instead made me feel like I was going to barf.

While Vivi and Thea ate, I half listened to the TV and half zoned out. For a brief moment, I wondered if my dad was still texting me. Or if he'd tried calling again. But I wasn't turning my phone back on tonight. I'd had quite enough of talking to people besides Vivi and Thea for today, thank you.

"I think I'm going to withdraw from the show," I said.

"Um, what?" Thea asked.

Vivi's brown eyes were wide when she looked over at me. "Yeah, *what*? Abby, you can't drop out!"

"How can I go tomorrow?" I asked. "I'll be there almost all day to compete and take care of Beau before and after. If my dad were coming, it would be different. But now . . . I'm going to run into Emery. There's no way around it. And Nina. I just don't know if it's worth it."

"Who cares if you run into them?" Thea asked. "They messed up. Not you. You shouldn't be the one nervous about seeing them again. They should be worried about seeing *you*."

"I totally agree." Vivi nodded. "Nina hurt you lots already, Abs. And Emery, too. But you can't let them have this. This would give Nina—and Selly, really—exactly what they want."

"I don't know," I said, sighing.

"The show season is tough enough," Thea said. "If you scratch, you'll regret it, Abby. I know you will. You'll never, ever forgive yourself for bowing out."

Vivi's eyes met mine. "And Beau did so well today. He deserves to finish the competition, and so do you."

"Ugggh," I said, moaning. "I don't want to face Nina. Or Emery. Especially alone!"

"You won't be alone," Thea said. "Hello, *I'll* be there all day."

"You'll be busy as team captain," I grumbled. Then, to make sure Thea knew I wasn't truly salty about it, I said, "But you know I'm not mad about that. At all. It's the situation."

Thea touched my forearm. "I know, silly."

"I feel like crap, and I want to hide in my bed all day tomorrow."

I saw Thea's and Vivi's eyes connect as they looked over me.

"Don't try to come up with a plan," I warned them. "I'll text Rebecca in the morning. I'm not going."

"Okay, wait. Hold your horses," Vivi said. "No pun intended."

I laughed despite myself.

"I don't have anything going on tomorrow," Vivi continued. "What if I come?"

I sat up so I could look at her. "Are you serious?"

"Abby, would I joke about coming and then say I was kidding? Especially tonight? I don't think so."

Vivi gave me a soft smile, and tears pricked my eyes.

I leaned over and wrapped my arms around her neck. She squeezed me back, hard. "Is that a yes?" she asked.

"Yes! Obviously!"

"This is going to be fun," Thea said.

Vivi jumped up, nearly sprinting to her closet. She flung open the door and started rummaging around inside.

"What's she doing?" I asked Thea.

"No idea." Thea called to Vivi, "Are you looking for a horsey outfit for tomorrow?"

"You'll see!" was Vivi's muffled reply.

Suddenly, random pants, a balled-up sweatshirt, and a school baseball cap came flying out of the closet.

Vivi emerged, a triumphant grin on her face. "Abby, I'm going to be your dad tomorrow!"

"*What?*"

Vivi stuck out her tongue at me. "Look, I've got my foam finger to cheer you on." She slid her hand into it and waved it around. "Woo, go, Abby! Ride Beau! Make him jump that fence!"

Thea and I burst into laughter.

"And I've got my trusty dad baseball cap," Vivi said, putting on a Saddlehill hat.

"This is amazing," I said to Thea.

"The most amazing," she said.

Neither of us took our eyes off Vivi as she grabbed her makeup bag and looked through it. With a smile, she pulled out an eyebrow pencil and turned away from us as she stared into her mirror.

"What's she doing now?" I stage-whispered to Thea.

Abby Obviously

EARLY SATURDAY MORNING, I WAS BACK at the stable for day two of the three-day event. Thea and I stepped off the bus, heading for the barn, and I looked around—wary of seeing Emery or Nina. But thankfully, I didn't see either of them.

Thea nudged my arm with hers. "It's going to be okay," she said. "Promise. We'll stick together as much as possible and get the horses ready."

"Then Vivi will be here," I said, "and I'll be super distracted with that."

"Not a clue!"

Vivi turned back around, looking at us with the most innocent look ever on her face. "Now I'm a dad."

"Oh my god," I said.

Vivi had used her eyebrow pencil to draw a very uneven, very ridiculous-looking mustache on her upper lip.

"I can't wait to show up tomorrow just like this!" she squealed, touching the brim of her hat.

We started laughing, and it was a long minute before we stopped.

"Exactly. And let's hope she really and truly does not show up in her dad outfit."

"I don't trust her," I joked. "She's probably adding to it now and making it even more ridiculous."

Thea laughed. "Probs."

"Want to say hi to the horses, then go walk the course?" I asked.

"Absolutely."

We walked into the mostly empty barn and meandered down to Beau's stall, and I peeked in on my bay gelding. "Hi, beautiful."

He whickered and came up to me, pushing his nose over the stall door and toward my hands. His black chin whiskers tickled my palm.

"Did you sleep okay?" I asked him.

He bobbed his head as if to say yes, he had.

"Thea and I are going to tell Chaos good morning and walk the course," I said. "Then I'll be back to get you tacked up and ready for our safety check, okay?"

I dropped a kiss on Beau's muzzle, and Thea reached over and patted his cheek.

She looped an arm in mine as we walked down to Chaos's stall and peered inside. He was still sound asleep this early in

the morning. Most of the other horses were too, and the barn was pretty quiet.

My stomach flipped as boots shuffled down the aisle, but it was a guy I didn't know and thankfully not Emery or Nina.

"Good morning, handsome," Thea whispered, trying to gently wake up Chaos. But he didn't move. Not so much as even an ear flick in our direction.

"Psst, Chaos Gremlin, wake up," she tried again. "It's jumping day."

That did it. The bright chestnut gelding turned both ears toward Thea and blinked sleepily, peeking at us through long eyelashes.

We giggled as he did a full-body shudder to shake off the sleep and came over to us to say hi.

"He just gets more and more handsome," I said. "Every time I look at him, it makes me want a chestnut too."

Chaos stuck his muzzle out to me, and I stroked the velvety softness.

"Maybe one day, we'll have two horses," Thea said. "Or three!"

I shook my head. "Oh, no. No thank you. One is plenty."

She laughed, and together, we walked to arena D, where the jumping course was set up. We walked the course, counting

strides and looking for the best path to take our horses. As we walked, more riders joined us. We moved methodically from jump to jump, pausing, thinking, counting.

The jumps were all decked out for fall, with brightly colored ribbons, spray-painted tree branches, and lots of fake flowers.

"What do you think?" Thea asked.

"It's not bad," I said. "Not bad at all. It's a pretty straight-forward course."

"Yeah, there's nothing I'm too worried about. At least, not right now. I'll probably walk away, start overthinking it, and then convince myself I'm going to mess it up."

"You won't. This is going to be a great round for you."

Thea and I traded smiles.

Beau would like this course—I could tell already. There was a nice mix of verticals and oxers with a couple of combos. Nothing too tricky. As I walked to the last jump, I crossed my fingers that we'd do as well or better today than we'd done yesterday. I wanted to keep our team placement ahead of Selly's.

Thea and I started out of the arena, and I looked up just in time to come face-to-face with Emery.

Her eyes widened when she saw me, and she tucked a lock of her honey-blond hair behind her ear. "Abby—"

"I don't want to talk," I said.

"Please," Emery said as she walked toward me. "Just give me one minute."

"No," I snapped. My voice rose with each word. "I have nothing to say to you."

Thea looked nervously between us. "Hey, don't yell," she pleaded. "If you two are going to talk, get away from the arena before Rebecca hears you."

I shook my head. "We're not going to talk." I turned back to Emery. "Leave me alone. I'm serious."

"Abby, we're both competing this weekend. And we'll run into each other at Saddlehill."

"Just because we're here doesn't mean we're going to talk. Why aren't you hanging out with Selly and Nina, since you so desperately want to be their friend?"

"I don't! I never wanted that, especially not with Nina. Not when I—"

I waved a hand, cutting her off. "Emery, just stop." I took a breath, then spit out, "I want to pretend you don't even exist."

Emery's cheeks turned pink and splotchy as her face fell. She hung her head and let me pass by her without another word.

With Thea on my heels, I hurried away from the arena.

"I hate this," I said to Thea. "I hate feeling like I'm the one who did something wrong here."

"You didn't. But I wish you didn't feel as though you had to duck and run from Emery."

I frowned. "It's not so much running as it is that I don't want to talk to her. At all." Anger flared hot in my chest. "After those sad texts she sent me yesterday that we all read, that was it."

"She needs to leave you alone, at the very least," Thea said. "You don't want to talk to her right now. She shouldn't try to force it, especially not during a show. Everyone's trying to get in the zone and focus. There's not much room to think about other stuff."

Thea was right. On the heels of my lackluster season last year, all I wanted was time to shine. And that wasn't going to happen if I was distracted—again—by everything around me. I had to stay focused on my rides and on Beau. I was determined not to mess up this show season for us.

We stopped just shy of the stable to watch a girl struggle with a very jittery mare. The pretty gray threw her head into the air and jerked back as she tried to rear, and I winced, imagining the lead rope burning through the girl's hands as she tried to keep the mare still despite her repeated head tossing.

I looked around for Rebecca or Allie, another Foxbury instructor, but they were nowhere to be seen.

"Maybe she needs help," I murmured to Thea. The mare shied violently, her nostrils flaring as the girl tried to walk her in tight circles.

Slowly, so we didn't spook the horse, we walked toward them.

"Do you need anything?" Thea called, her voice gentle.

"Thanks, but I think I'm okay," the girl said, her red hair sticking to her forehead. "Actually, is there a round pen nearby? I'd love to lunge her for a bit and work out some of her energy."

And, of course, just as she said that, her mare calmed down and blinked at us with an innocent look.

"I can take you over there," Thea said. "There's a shortcut."

"That would be super," the girl said, giving us a grateful smile.

It felt like she was smiling only at me, and it made the tips of my ears burn. I realized she was cute. Really cute.

Thea glanced at me, then back at the new girl. "Oh, shoot," Thea said. "I forgot! I have . . . team captain stuff."

"No, you don't," I said. What was she talking about?

"Yes, I do," Thea said, shooting me a look before turning to the other girl. "But don't worry, Abby will take you!"

A furious blush crept over my face. "I'm—I'm Abby. Obviously."

"Hi, Abby Obviously. I'm Mila Bloom."

"My last name's actually not 'Obviously,'" I blurted out. "It's St. Clair."

Mila laughed. "I figured! I was just teasing you."

Abby, you absolute idiot! Of course she was.

"Let me help with your mare," I said, hurrying around to the horse's other side just as the mare began to dance in place. It was safe here. Mila couldn't see my face! It was definitely red. And I was *definitely* sweaty for no apparent reason. I grabbed the mare's halter, cooing to her as I pointed us in the direction of the round pen.

"This prancing wild thing is Circe," Mila said. "She's not usually like this, I swear!"

"Hi, Circe," I said. "I'd love to pet you once you're calmer."

The mare tugged us forward with a snort. She wasn't going to let me do that anytime soon!

"There's the round pen," I said, trying not to pant, but this was not easy.

We let Circe trot between us, hurrying her inside the pen. Once she was safely inside with Mila, I closed the gate and joined them in the center of the pen. Mila swapped the lead rope for the lunge line she'd been carrying and fed the line to Circe. The mare broke into a quick trot and circled us.

"Thank you so, so much," Mila said. "We wouldn't have made it over here."

I waved my hand. "You totally would have. It just would have been a little more difficult." I looked down at my boots, then back at Circe, watching her trot. "Are you new here? I mean, you must be. I've never seen you before." The words tumbled out of my mouth ridiculously fast. "Not that I was looking for you or anything!"

Mila laughed, flicking her green eyes to me and then back to her horse.

"I'm going to stop talking now," I mumbled. I wished I could crumble into the arena dirt and never be seen again. Like, ever.

"We *are* new. Coming during a show weekend wasn't the smartest decision, but I'm transferring to Foxbury from Ainsley Stables." Mila frowned. "We had a bad fire, and it's going to take time to rebuild."

"Oh my god, a fire?! That's awful." A sick feeling crept over my stomach. "Barn fires are one of my worst nightmares. Were any horses or people hurt?"

"Thankfully, no. The grooms on night duty managed to get all the horses out of the stable and loose in the pastures before it got to them. A good portion of the barn is gone, yeah, but thinking about what we could have lost?" Mila shuddered. "I'll take losing my stuff over losing Circe any day."

"Do you need anything? If you need brushes or blankets or anything, really, just let me know. If I don't have extra of something to spare, I'm sure I can find someone who does."

She smiled. "Thanks! I appreciate that. I think we have everything we need right now, but I'll let you know if I think of anything."

"Okay, good. Are you joining a riding team?"

"Yeah! I'm trying out for Rebecca's middle novice team soon!"

"No way! I'm on the middle novice team!"

Anyone who proved their skills could join the middle novice team, but the more experienced team after mine had a set number of seats, and riders had to fight for them.

"Really? That's awesome! It will be so nice to know someone. If I make the team, of course."

"I'm sure you'll do great at tryouts. Rebecca's tough but fair."

"Good to know. Hopefully, I'll see you at practice one of these days."

When Mila asked Circe to change direction, the gray mare had finally calmed down. She put her black muzzle into Mila's hands and got a kiss on the cheek. Those two were really, really cute together. Supercute, in fact. Then I realized I was staring and shook my head a little, trying to clear my thoughts.

"I better go get ready for jumping," I said a bit reluctantly. "But I'll see you around."

"Good luck!" Mila flashed a smile at me, and a dimple appeared on one of her cheeks. "And yeah, see you around, Abby Obviously."

I smiled back before letting myself out of the round pen, my fingers fumbling on the latch.

The stable was busy now, as more riders had arrived for show day. The horses were awake now too, and so many beautiful heads were stuck out over stall doors.

I went to Beau's stall and slipped inside, wrapping my arms around his neck as I inhaled his familiar scent. It was truly one of the most calming scents in the entire world, and I needed all the chill I could get before today kicked off. All the chill I could get after meeting Mila.

Fantastic, Fabulous, and Ready to Kick Butt

A FTER BEAU WAS ALL TACKED UP AND ready to go, I changed into my show clothes, and we completed our safety check. I'd managed to find my focus, which was a major relief.

I led him down the aisle, halting him in front of the mirror and taking one last look at myself. My boots had a soft gleam, my breeches were spotless, and my jacket was pressed and clean.

You can do this, I told myself.

I led Beau out of the barn and down toward one of the warm-up arenas. The sun was bright, the September air was warm, and I shaded my eyes with my hand. And there, standing along the rail and waving wildly at us, was Vivi. Thankfully, she'd left the dad clothes at school.

I grinned, clucking to Beau as we hurried over to her. Beau seemed to have an extra bounce in his step. He could feel my excitement at having her here.

"You found the right arena and everything!" I said as we reached Vivi.

"I did! I'm so proud of myself right now. I got off the bus and followed the signs just like you told me." She smiled. Then she looked me up and down, taking in my show clothes. "You look fantastic, wow!"

"Fancy, right?"

"Very. Not like the clothes you come home from lessons in."

I laughed. "It would be a little much to ride in this jacket every day."

"True, true."

Beau reached his head toward Vivi, offering his nose for a pat.

"Can I pet him?" she asked, looking at me.

"Of course! I know you haven't seen him in a while, but he's still the same friendly guy."

Vivi had come to the stable with me a couple of times last year to hang out and watch me practice, but it had been months and months.

Slowly, she reached up and touched Beau's muzzle, letting him sniff her hand. He lowered his head so she could reach his forehead, and she gave him some scratches.

"Aww, he remembers me," she said.

"You're kind of hard to forget, you know."

That made Vivi smile.

"How's it going?" she asked.

"Um, well. It's been a bit of a day already. But I'll tell you about that later. Right now, I'm in focus mode."

"Oh yes! Don't let me interrupt."

"Do you want to watch us warm up, or do you want to go sit in the stands? Other riders are competing, so you could watch them if a warm-up isn't your thing."

"I came here for you," she said. "As long as I'm not distracting."

"Not at all."

She moved out of the way, leaning against the fence rails as I checked Beau's girth, then mounted and rode him into the arena.

As we warmed up, he seemed to flick his tail with a little extra pizzazz, like he knew Vivi was here for us.

I let him walk around the arena, stretching his neck and back as we made a couple of slow laps. Then I asked him for a trot, and I posted to warm up.

As we made a large circle, I looked over and laughed at what I saw. Vivi, perched on the arena rail, had her phone sideways and in front of her, tongue out in the corner of her mouth, as she presumably recorded my warm-up.

"How do we look?" I asked, heading over to her. I slowed Beau to a walk and smiled.

"Fantastic, fabulous, and ready to kick butt!" Vivi said. She lowered her phone. "Seriously. You look so great up there, and Beau is so handsome. I'll send that video to my cloud so I can post online one day and be like, 'See? I knew her when!'"

"Oh, *stop*," I said. I grinned. "Beau feels really good, though. He's just about ready to go."

I urged him back into a trot and then asked for a slow canter. While I rocked along to his smooth gait, I couldn't help but feel today was going to be our day!

After our warm-up, Vivi headed to the stands while Beau and I went to the competition arena, only to find Selly and Nina waiting nearby.

"Good luck, teammie!"

I gritted my teeth at the sound of Nina's voice, pretending I didn't hear her. I reached down and adjusted one of my stirrup irons.

Hoofbeats approached as Nina and Selly came over on their horses.

"I *said*, 'Good luck, teammie,'" Nina said. "Did you not hear me?"

"Sorry," I lied. "I didn't. But thanks."

"I'd say good luck," Selly said, "but you're going to need more than that to beat me."

I stared straight ahead, not letting myself get dragged into a back-and-forth with her.

"Abby, gosh," Nina said, fake sweetness dripping from her tone. "Don't be rude to Selly."

My breath caught a little as I looked up at Nina. She smirked and let what she'd said hang in the air. It felt like a threat.

"Whatever," Selly said, giving Nina a look. "I really don't care if Abby ignores me or not."

"I do," Nina said. "She needs to act like a good teammate."

And there it was. The unspoken "or else" that dripped from Nina's words. This was how it was going to be. She was never going to let me forget what she had over me. She was going to use it to keep me in line.

My cheeks burned.

Last night, I'd gone over and over it in my mind, trying to figure out why Nina hadn't told Selly what she knew about what I'd done. But the more I thought about it, the more it was clear—Nina loved this. She loved the power she had over me. And this secret between us? It was something Nina had over Selly, too. Nina was usually the powerless one in their duo. But this put Nina in control.

"You all set, Abby?" Thea, ever my savior, hurried up to me, reaching under Beau's chin and holding his reins.

"Yup. I'm ready."

"You're going to do great," she said. "I know it! Just breathe and focus."

I nodded, my throat getting a little tight as I watched the rider before me finish a nearly flawless round. His horse only tapped one rail, and it had stayed in the cup. The pressure was on, but this was what I'd been working so hard for—a chance to show my stuff against everyone else.

I looked down at Thea, managing a smile, and then leaned forward to pat Beau's neck. "We're ready!"

Before Nina or Selly could say another word to me, I gathered my reins and rode toward the arena entrance.

You've come this far, I told myself. *Don't blow it now.*

Inside, I let Beau move from a trot into a canter and pointed him at the first jump. He moved smoothly under me, eager to get to the white-and-yellow vertical.

I rocked in the saddle to Beau's canter and counted three, two, one, *now*!

When I got to *now,* I lifted my butt out of the saddle and leaned forward, pushing my hands up along his neck. Beau snapped his knees and tucked his forelegs tight as we sailed over the jump and cantered on.

A few strides later, we popped over another vertical—this one with red-and-white poles—and made a turn toward a pair of oxers decked out for fall with branches and leaves that could freak out Beau. I kept my leg on and made sure he stayed straight as we approached. He didn't wobble and sailed over it without a hitch.

I let Beau out a hair as we headed for a third vertical. His stride got a little long, and I worked to collect him and get the correct stride length back as we reached the jump. As we soared into the air, I smiled at the rush. This was the best feeling in the world! There was nothing like flying with your horse. The horse trusted the rider to guide them over the obstacle, and the rider trusted the horse to listen and give it their all.

Beau did everything with so much heart, and this ride was no exception. It was one of the reasons why he was my heart horse.

Beau leaped over the first oxer, and we cantered toward the next. As we made our way toward it, a slight breeze kicked up and Beau seemed to feel fall was coming. With a snort, he tossed his head. I let him get it out of his system, and within a couple of strides, he was back to being Profesh Beau.

We hopped over the next leaf-themed oxer, and I let Beau out a tiny bit as we swept into a turn at the arena's end and jumped a blue-and-white oxer with a wider spread.

We lined up for a combination, and I held my breath as he soared over the first, cantered one stride, and launched right back into the air for the second half of the combo.

Daaang it! I winced at the thud when one of Beau's back hooves whacked the rail just before we hit the ground.

I kept an ear trained toward it, listening for the telltale thunk of it coming out of the cup and hitting the ground, but it stayed up!

Yes, yes, yesss!

Two more to go. We could do this!

I listened to Beau's breathing and felt him under me—he wasn't tired yet, I could tell. So I let my reins out a bit more to give him enough speed to get over the final two verticals.

Beau cantered up to the next-to-last vertical—one with wooden horse heads at the ends—and leaped over it without hesitation.

We turned toward the final vertical, and he tossed his head.

Calm down, boy, we're almost done, I thought.

I got him quieter right as the jump rushed at us, but it wasn't enough. Beau wasn't paying attention when he popped over the orange-and-purple rails, and I knew we were too early on takeoff.

No, no, no!

Just before we landed, his back hoof tapped the rail, and it thundered to the ground behind us.

I kept my chin up as I sat deep in the saddle, letting Beau canter for a few strides before bringing him to a trot. I leaned forward and patted his neck.

"Good job, boy!"

Four faults weren't too bad, but still. I *really* wished we'd gone clean. I tried to tell myself it was only one rail at our first show back for the season, and I shouldn't be mad about it.

"YAAAAY, BESTIE!"

I didn't have to look toward the stands to know exactly who that was.

"THAT'S MY BEST FRIEND!"

Oh my *god*. Vivi was out of control!

Laughing, I waved in her direction before turning Beau toward the exit. Her enthusiasm was an insta–mood booster. I was so excited that she was here, and I'd gotten the okay from Rebecca to have her hang out with me back in the stable too, as long as I kept her out of the way of other riders.

"You did great," I told Beau. "I'm really proud of you!"

I trotted him through the exit, riding him over to a waiting Thea.

"Dude," Thea said, laughing. "I could hear Vivi down here."

I laughed too, sliding out of Beau's saddle. "She's wild, that one. But she's always got my back."

"We love a supportive best friend," Thea said. "And speaking of support, YAY! You rocked that!"

I loosened Beau's girth and patted his shoulder. "We did okay! I wish we'd gone clean, obviously. But for our first show back, we did all right."

"You did *very* well. A great score for our team."

And, for the first time today, I was happy. The relief of the ride being over—phase two out of three was down—and we had one more phase to go tomorrow.

We moved away from the arena so I could cool Beau. But before I'd gotten too far, someone loudly whispered my name.

"Abbyyy, wait!"

I looked behind me, shaking my head as I watched Vivi walk comically slow toward us. "What are you doing?"

"You're not supposed to run around horses!"

Laughing, Thea and I stopped so Vivi could catch up to us.

"This is true," I said. "But you can also walk faster than that. I promise Beau won't mind."

Vivi finally reached us and hugged me. "That ride! Wow, you two jumped so high! And you didn't fall off!"

"Thankfully!" I said.

"And Beau *ran* in between those jumps," Vivi said, eyes slightly wide. "He's fast!"

"That's only his canter too," I said. "Wait until you see him gallop one day."

"He goes . . . faster?"

"Yup."

"Wow," Vivi said. "He looked very fast to me!"

I laughed, patting Beau's shoulder. "He was fast, yes, but not even close to top speed."

Thea glanced at her phone. "Hey, I've got to go back and be there for Nina's ride in a sec. But . . ."

"Oh, yes," Vivi said. "There's a 'but.' And that is—we want to tell you something first!"

"Um, I'm not sure if I can handle any more surprises today," I said. "You're making me nervous!"

"It's not bad!" Thea said. "Don't be worried."

"And it's nothing huge," Vivi said. "But Thea and I have been talking, and we sort of planned a night out for the three of us."

"What?" I was so confused.

"We made dinner reservations," Thea said. "After, we can get ice cream and walk on the beach."

"Then we'll come back to school, get into pj's, and watch a horror movie," Vivi said.

"Are you in?" Thea asked.

"Am I in? Am I *in*? You didn't have to do this." Still holding on to Beau's reins with one hand, I moved so I could put an arm around each of my friends. "This is the best surprise ever!"

Thea and Vivi traded relief-filled smiles with each other.

"We thought you'd like it," Vivi said, "but then we got a little nervous. Like, what if you just wanted to hang in our room tonight and chill?"

I shook my head. "No way! I want to go out, and it'll help keep my mind off stuff."

Beau snorted, nudging my arm as if to agree.

"You've got one more phase of the competition," Thea said. "And hopefully, tonight will help you relax and have fun."

"It's going to be great." I smiled. "Exactly what I need before cross-country."

Vivi reached over and patted Beau's neck. He shut his eyes for a second, leaning into her hand.

I hugged Vivi, squeezing her extra tight before letting go. "Thank you so much for coming. Not to sound cheesy, but it meant the world to me. And thank you for tonight. You and Thea are the best."

Vivi smiled. "You're welcome. Tonight's gonna be so much fun!"

"I don't want to," Thea said, "but I really have to go check on Nina and support her like a team captain."

I wrinkled my nose. "Ugh, but I get it. Go do your thing, and Vivi'll keep me company for a bit, right?"

She nodded. "Of course! I'm not ready to go back to school yet."

"Text me if you need anything," Thea said to us. "I'm going to be running around, but I'll check my phone when I can."

Vivi and I waved to Thea. Then we headed off down one of the shady lanes to walk Beau. Despite everything that had happened yesterday, this show was turning around.

Sasha Silver Sleep Technique

A COUPLE OF HOURS LATER, I WAS DONE for the day. Vivi had gone back to school, and I'd walked the cross-country course and tidied up around Beau's stall a bit—wanting to make sure I got a perfect mount management score—and checked his water bucket once more. Then I hopped on the bus and headed to Saddlehill.

Vivi was out, probably getting errands done before tonight, and I hurried through showering and getting ready. This night with my friends was exactly what I needed.

A notification flashed in my group chat with Thea and Vivi.

Thea: I'm back at school! Showering then I'll be over :)

Abby: Yesss! Can't wait

I stretched out on top of my bed, just to rest for a few minutes. I'd been up so early, and horse shows were exhausting. Especially three-day events. They were super high-stress, from riding to making sure everything was perfect in the stable and with Beau's tack and care. It felt like I was constantly "on" to make sure it all went well. And having to dodge Emery and deal with Nina hadn't made the weekend any easier.

At least tomorrow is it, I told myself. Then I would have a little time to think over what I needed to do about Nina. I wasn't sure what there was *to* do, exactly. If I went to Rebecca and told her what I'd done, what would happen to me? Would she kick me off the Interscholastic Pony League team forever?

Even thinking about that possibility made my heart race a little. There seemed to be no right answers in this situation.

I closed my eyes and laid my forearm across them. I'd read in an interview with Sasha Silver that she liked to practice yoga breathing when she was in a stressful situation. Years ago, Sasha had been a rider for a rival boarding school, Canterwood Crest. Now she was competing in pre-Olympic trials and teaching up-and-coming riders.

Deep breath in, deep breath out. I tried it, concentrating on finding my zen.

In and out.

In and out.

"Abby?"

I pulled my arm off my eyes, looked over, and saw Vivi smiling at me. I sat up with a jolt.

"You scared me! I didn't even hear you come in!" I said, rubbing my eyes.

"That's because you were snoring," Thea said from Vivi's desk chair.

"What? Are you sure?"

"Pretty sure," Thea said. "Unless you snore while you're awake? And if so, you should probably get that checked out."

I laughed, guessing Sasha's breathing techniques had worked. I hadn't even realized I'd fallen asleep!

"We got here about ten minutes ago, and you were out cold," Vivi explained. "We let you sleep for a few, but then we couldn't wait."

Thea nodded, her eyes all lit up with excitement. "You can sleep later, because I'm starving! Ready to go?"

"Yesss! I'm so ready." I hopped off my bed and smoothed

my hands over my pants, making sure my clothes weren't wrinkled from my impromptu nap.

"Wait," I said, "I'm dressed okay, right? You haven't told me where we're going for dinner."

Vivi and Thea nodded.

"You're good," Thea said. "It's a casual place."

With that, I grabbed my plum-colored jacket in case it got windy by the beach later and hurried out the door behind my friends.

Once we were all signed out, we climbed into one of the school vans, and it dropped us off on the far east side of Foxbury, which was right on the beach. A gentle breeze lifted my hair off my neck, and I sighed happily. I loved everything about coming here. From the salty air to the seagulls that hopped along the boardwalk to the porpoises I'd spot on occasion as they frolicked in the water.

The beach felt full of possibility. I never knew what I could find along the shore, and every walk on the beach was an adventure. Plus, dining on the beach felt oh-so-fancy and made me feel very grown-up. And coming here with my two best friends made it all that much more special.

Together, the three of us wound our way through the small downtown area, heading for the strip of beach that was dotted with shops and restaurants. The beachfront wasn't that busy for a weekend evening, and it felt so good to be away from campus and the stable.

"The chances that we'll run into anyone from school are slim," I said, "and I know they're not zero, but still. They're not great. And that feels amazing."

"Agreed," Thea said.

"You know what's even more amazing?" Vivi asked. "Reservations for this one place were hard to get." She pouted. "But I kept checking and checking and finally snagged them last-minute!" Her pout transformed into a grin.

"Nooo," I said. "Tell me we're not going to Shores?"

"We're going to Shores!" Thea said.

"The best seafood and house-made pasta will be ours," Vivi declared.

"This is where I wanted to come with my dad," I said, "so I'm glad I get to go with you two."

Thea smiled. "Good. I promise, we're going to have a great time. And hey, when you do come here with your dad, you'll already know the menu."

I nodded. "True."

Shores was *the* place to come for a fresh seaside meal. So many people at school had talked about it, and it had made me really want to go. But I'd never found the right time. Until now, apparently.

We stepped inside, and I couldn't help but stare. So many of the walls were solid glass, and they offered a panoramic view of the Atlantic Ocean. All the lighting fixtures were eye-catching copper wires with bare light bulbs hanging down at various heights. On the wall was a giant mural of a colorful and vibrant swordfish.

"This place is so cool," I said in a whisper.

A waiter came over, took our names, and led us to our table, which had a perfect view of the water. I slid into a navy-blue booth, with Vivi next to me and Thea across from us.

Once the waiter poured our glasses of water and took our orders of three Sprites, we turned toward the ocean, and I smiled.

"I'm glad we could go now," Thea said. "Soon, things are going to be ridiculously busy as we get further into the semester. My teachers are already starting to assign more homework, and we haven't even started the second week of classes."

"Mine, too," I said. "We should probably start up last year's study group with Ankita and Willa."

My friends nodded.

"Let's all scoot to the end of the booth and get a pic with the ocean in the background!" Vivi said.

We did, grinning at the camera as I snapped a picture of us.

"I'm going to post it," I said.

"Do it. We look adorable," Thea said.

I posted the pic, tagging Thea and Vivi. I hadn't even put down my phone when I got a *1 new like* notification.

Emery Flynn liked your photo.

"Really?" I muttered.

"What?" Thea asked.

I held up my phone so she and Vivi could see my screen.

Thea rolled her eyes. "Whatever. She can like your pics all she wants. At least she sees you're out having a great time, and you're not sitting around and waiting for her apology."

"Exactly." I put my phone facedown on the table. "No more talking about her. Not tonight, anyway. I want to have fun and not think about Emery."

"We got you," Vivi said, grinning. "Fun it is!"

Heart Eyes? Me?

THE WAITER BROUGHT OUR DRINKS, and we ordered a mini-crab-cakes appetizer to split while we browsed the menu and looked at the ocean. The waves gently lapped the shore and rocked a few of the docked sailboats. If I squinted, I could see boats far out on the water.

Thea smiled at me and Vivi. "The sunset is going to be beautiful, I bet."

"We have the best place to see it too," Vivi said.

I stole a glance at Thea across the table, then one at Vivi

next to me. Sure, this evening wasn't at all what I'd thought it was going to be. I thought I'd come to Shores first with my dad, then later with my friends. This weekend was supposed to be about me and Dad. And the show, of course, but this night was what I'd been most looking forward to.

Who knew when I would see him next? He was always busier in the fall, and so was I with riding and school. *Maybe I'll be too busy for him,* I thought pettily, even though as I thought it I knew I would never, ever be too busy for my dad.

I picked up my menu again, browsing the sleek nautical-themed paper. My stomach growled a little as I considered all my options.

"This is hard," Thea said. "I want everything."

Vivi nodded. "So, we'll obviously have to come back."

"I want it all too," I said. "I'm going for the tuna poke bowl."

"It's the New England clam chowder for me," Thea said. "I haven't had it in so long."

"Mushroom gnocchi here," Vivi said.

The waiter came back and took our orders, and I tried to ignore my hungry stomach. It smelled so good in here. Wafts of fresh seafood kept hitting my nose.

"It's starting to feel like fall," Thea said. "Even though it's not, technically."

"Speaking of fall, I can't believe the harvest dance is coming up!" Vivi said.

"Me either. And we know you're going with Asher," I said, wiggling my eyebrows.

"How do you know?" she asked. "I don't even know this!"

Thea and I laughed.

"It's kind of obvious," Thea said. "He's so gonna ask you."

Vivi grinned. "I hope so. Or I'll ask him. If he says yes, I'll dance with him and hang out some, but I'll def hang with you all too."

"Abby, however, will *not* have plenty of time for her friends," Thea said, giving me a sly smile.

"What?" Vivi asked. Her mouth hung open a little, and she looked back and forth between the two of us.

"Yeah, what?!" I added.

"You're totally asking Mila," Thea said. "You have the biggest heart eyes ever for her."

"Who is *Mila*? I don't know a Mila!" Vivi put down her drink and slapped her palms flat on the table. "Tell me!"

"It's nothing, omigod!" I grinned. "She's a new girl at the

stable. She's just transferred to Foxbury and is trying out for the middle novice team."

"See? You're already sharing info with each other." Thea gave us a satisfied, smug smile. "Mila didn't tell me any of that."

"Because Circe was trying to run us over!" I protested. "How could she have?"

"Mm-hmm, suuure," Thea said.

"Is she cute?" Vivi asked.

A silly smile stretched from one of my ears to the other. Instead of answering, I took a giant gulp of soda.

"Okay, so she's very cute," Vivi said. "Got it."

"She has really bright green eyes," I finally said. "And they're really pretty. And she smiled at me. And I kind of forgot where I was."

Thea and Vivi did a little dance in their seats.

"This is so freaking adorable, I can't stand it," Thea said. "Your first real crush!"

"I've had crushes before," I pointed out. "Well, okay. On actors and singers and that one older girl from the pizza place I love in Fieldcrest. And that girl from my old barn." I tilted my head. "And do I even want to date boys? Some are cute, but I don't know! Maybe I just like girls."

"You don't have to know," Thea said. "You can date anyone you want. Or not! And maybe later, things will change. That's okay."

"Yeah," Vivi said. "I mean, right now, I like boys. But if I meet the right girl one day?" She shrugged. "Who knows?"

"I wonder what school Mila goes to," Thea said.

"Me too!" I said. "If I talk to her again, I'll ask. If I can. It's ridiculous. I try to say smart stuff, and it comes out all garbled and dumb!"

"That's definitely your crush brain speaking for you," Vivi said. "I did that when I first started talking to Asher. Everything came out way too fast!"

"Yes!" I nodded. "That's what happened to me! It was the *worst*. Oh my god, Mila probably thinks I'm an idiot."

"Doubt it," Thea said. "I saw the way she looked at you when we met. She thought you were cute too."

I laughed. "Thea, that's not what happened at all." I looked at Vivi. "I promise. Mila had zero time to even look in my direction until we got Circe to the round pen. And even then, she was busy."

"Then it's simple: you'll have to talk to her again when

~ 66 ~

Circe isn't tugging her around all over the place, and you'll be able to tell."

"Tell what?" I asked.

"If she'd like your number so you can ask her to the harvest dance. We're allowed to invite people from other schools!" Thea said, laughing.

"I'm not. I can't!" I couldn't form complete sentences. "It's next weekend."

"You can," Vivi said. "And yes, that's the perfect amount of time. Hang out with her again next week, then casually ask her if she wants to come to the dance."

"With me," I said.

"With you," Thea and Vivi said in unison.

"Even if you don't hit it off like that, you could make a new friend," Thea said. "Friends are always good!"

"Oh god, okay," I said. "I'll think about it. But she might not even like girls!"

Thea shook her head. "I'd be willing to bet Chaos that she does."

And before my friends could try and talk me into it even more, the waiter came with our meals.

"Enjoy!" he told us, setting down the plates.

And as we dug into our food, I couldn't help but smile as I imagined, just for a second, talking to Mila again.

"Well," Vivi said as we left the restaurant and were treated to a gorgeous sunset. "Our waiter told us to enjoy, but I should have enjoyed it a little less. I ate way too much!"

"Right?" Thea asked.

Thea and I laughed.

"The food was ridiculous," I said. "Thank you for bringing me here!"

"Of course!" Vivi said. "And it was really delish."

"My dessert stomach is still ready for ice cream, though," Thea said.

"Well, same," I said.

"Want to walk along the water for a bit and then get ice cream?" Vivi asked.

Thea and I nodded.

We headed away from the restaurant and down a path to the beach.

The three of us tugged off our socks and shoes, and I smiled when my bare feet hit the sand. "Walking on the beach is one of my all-time fave things to do," I said. "It's so chill."

The three of us linked arms as we walked. A gentle breeze kept me cool, and I felt content. Finally. We meandered down the shore, stopping every so often to pick up a pretty shell.

"Is this someone's job?" I asked. "Hunting shells and looking for sea glass? Because if so, I might give up on the whole professional equestrian thing and do this."

"Or merge them," Thea said, bending down to grab a scallop shell. "You could be a professional equestrian who rides her horse up and down various beaches and collects shells."

"Ooh, you're onto something!" I smiled. "In that case, I better get Beau over his water phobia ASAP, since we're going to be spending a lot of time at the beach."

"You two need to get sponsored by a travel company," Vivi said. "Then you'd get free trips to take me on." She grinned at us.

"Sasha Silver and Heather Fox *have* been sponsored since high school," I said slowly, thinking of the two prominent Canterwood Crest riders.

"Sasha's got the beauty-box deal, and Heather's with TKEQ," Thea said.

"The horsey clothing shop you buy a zillion things a month from?" Vivi asked.

I nodded. TKEQ had the *best* equestrian clothes. They even had a new line of hoodies modeled by Heather. They were *very* back-ordered now, of course, and it would be months before I got mine.

My phone buzzed, and I checked to see a new text.

It was Dad.

A Dinner Surprise

I SIGHED, ROLLING MY EYES. "MY DAD WANTS to talk."

"You told him you would, right?" Vivi asked.

I nodded. "I still don't want to talk to him, though."

"I wouldn't either, but get it out of the way," Thea said. "Then you won't have to think about it tonight."

"Thea and I will go check out that ice cream stand." Vivi tipped her chin toward a beachside ice cream stand a few yards ahead. "Meet us there when you're done?"

"Okay, okay." I sighed. "I'll just be a minute."

I texted Dad back.

Abby: Can I call you now?

Dad: Of course!

Taking a deep breath, I called, and he answered on the first ring.

"Hey, honey," he said.

"Hi."

"I can tell that you're still upset," he said. "And Abs, you have every right to be. I should have been there for you this weekend, and I'm not. I"—he hesitated—"I made the wrong decision, and I'm sorry. There's no excuse for not being there for my kid."

Wow. Tears burned my eyes. I'd hoped he would apologize, since he was usually quick to apologize when he was wrong, but I could actually hear in his voice how sorry he was.

"Thanks," I said, still wanting him to do the talking.

"Abby, it's upsetting that you don't know how important you are to me. I know when we talked, I tried to make this about our new family, but it's not. It's about you and me."

"Yeah," I said, softening. "It's really not about Natalie or Emery, Dad. You promised you'd be here. And this weekend is a big deal."

"I know it is. You're so independent. But I need to remember that you're twelve. You need me sometimes too, and you count on me and want me around."

"It's just . . . it's the first show of the season. I know I show a lot during the year. And I don't expect you to come to all of them!" I added quickly. "But the first one back was a huge one for me, especially after how things went downhill last show season." I paused, thinking for a second. "I needed your support."

"Yes, yes, you did. I'm so sorry I let you down. I mean it, Abby. I made the wrong choice this weekend. I want to make it up to you."

I rubbed my forehead. I hadn't expected the conversation to go like this at all. I'd been pretty set on staying mad at him.

"Thanks, Dad. You don't need to make it up to me or anything, but please, next time you say you're coming—show up, okay?"

"You have my word. And speaking of which, I'm giving it to you now—my word—that I'll be in town tomorrow evening."

"What?"

"I rearranged some things. You were right, Abs. I'm the

boss, and this is important to me. It won't be until later, but I planned a Sunday dinner for all of us!" I could feel the smile on Dad's face. "You, me, Emery, and Natalie. I got last-minute reservations at a great steak house with tons of vegetarian options in case you or Emery don't want steak."

Oh.

No.

Judging by the tone of Dad's voice and our convo so far, I didn't think he had any clue that Emery and I weren't speaking.

"Dinner sounds . . . good," I said cautiously.

"I can't wait to see you, hon. And hey, how did it go today?" Dad asked. "Natalie and I talked earlier, and she said you did really well."

"It wasn't a bad day. Nothing spectacular, but we didn't make any major mistakes aside from knocking a rail. I wish we'd gone clear, but I'll take it for the first show of the season."

"And tomorrow's cross-country," Dad said. "Is Beau rested?"

"I think so. He seemed fine after jumping, and I think he'll get a good night's sleep and then be all ready to go tomorrow."

"Did you walk the course?"

"Yup. It's got a few tricky spots."

"Pffft," Dad said. "I know you'll handle them just fine."

"We'll see! I hope so."

We stayed on the phone for a couple more minutes before I told him I needed to go hang with Thea and Vivi.

"I love you, Abs. I'll see you tomorrow, okay?"

"Love you, too. And okay, Dad. Can't wait to see you."

I hung up, feeling relief sweep over me as I headed toward my friends. The call hadn't been something I'd wanted to do, but now I was glad I had. The only tricky part? That dinner with Emery.

"How'd it go?" Vivi asked. She had an ice cream cone in each hand.

"Good, actually," I said. "He's sorry, and I'm glad we talked. But he's coming tomorrow evening for dinner."

"Yay!" Thea said.

"Wait, why don't you look happier?" Vivi asked.

"Well, he's inviting Natalie and Emery."

"Oh, crap," Thea said.

"That's going to be so awkward," Vivi said. "Sorry, Abs."

I sighed. "I'm not looking forward to Emery being there. But I don't want my dad to know there's anything going on." I looked from Thea to Vivi and back again. "Forget about me for a moment—I'd say things went really well for *you*." I nodded to the ice cream. "What've you got there? And is one for me?"

Vivi grinned. "Um, no?" She darted around me as I reached for a cone. "I wanted to sample these!"

"Sample?" I asked, laughing. "Those are full size!"

"Yes, sample the full sizes!"

Shaking my head, I turned to Thea. "Can you believe . . ." I didn't finish my sentence as I eyed what was in Thea's hands. "You too, huh?" I asked.

She laughed. "We weren't sure how long you would be. So two ice creams each sounded very appropriate."

"Oh, I'm here for it," I said. "I'm going to get two!"

I glanced over the menu, taking way too long to decide, but finally, I stepped away with a cone in each hand. One chocolate with marshmallow topping and one maple swirl.

Together, Vivi, Thea, and I wandered down the beach, eating our cones and watching the ocean.

"We've got so many great things coming up soon," Vivi said, "well, soonish. Like, Halloween in—"

"Salem!" Thea and I said at the same time.

This year, Saddlehill was driving students to an off-campus Halloween bash in spooky, historic Salem.

We kept walking along the beach, taking in the chill atmosphere and looking hard for any harbor porpoises. But the beach was quiet aside from a jumping fish here or there. We wound our way down the shore, climbing up a rocky area to peer into a tide pool.

Inside the shallow water, a few tiny hermit crabs combed the rocks. I bent down to get a closer look and snapped a pic of one with a pretty shell.

"Look over here," Thea said. "A little mussel or something is hiding under that rock."

Vivi and I went over and crouched down next to Thea, and the three of us watched the teensy mussel blow bubbles out from its hiding place. As I watched the mussel, I couldn't help but relate. I felt as though I were hiding this weekend—from Nina and kind of from Emery—and blowing out bubbles of nervous energy.

But as I glanced over at my friends, I knew what I had to do: I had to stay focused on what I wanted more than anything—winning. And that meant I wasn't going to put a single ounce of energy toward hiding.

From *anyone*.

Ask the Cards

BACK IN VIVI'S AND MY ROOM, I
squished down even more under my blanket as
the movie started. We'd turned off the lights, save
for the row of fairy lights along the mantel and a couple of
caramel-scented candles Vivi had lit. For the first time this
weekend, I felt as though I could truly, 100 percent relax.
I didn't care what Emery was doing with her mom, and
Nina wasn't on my mind. Usually, I'd be worrying about
cross-country by now, but even that wasn't something I was
thinking about.

Instead, I got lost in the movie, jumping when a demonic spirit chased the heroine out of her house and into the streets, screaming.

"Run, run, run," Vivi chanted under her breath.

"Don't go in there!" Thea said.

I groaned. "That's the biggest mistake ever. The spirit will follow her in there, and she's going to be trapped!"

I held my breath, hoping I was wrong. We shrieked when the demon flew into the garage where the girl had run, and Thea covered her eyes with her hands.

We fell silent, peeping over the tops of our blankets and holding our breath as we watched.

When we finally got to a lull in the scares, we paused the movie, and Thea and Vivi went downstairs to the kitchen to get snacks and sodas.

I browsed TikTok, then checked Instagram and scrolled my friends' pictures. I passed one photo a little too fast, so I went back up to look again. It was a pic of Emery, smiling as she stood in front of a giant sign that pointed to a sunflower maze. *Chill weekend with Mom!* it was captioned.

I stared at the photo for too long, zooming in and really looking at Emery's face for any trace of remorse or sadness about what she'd done. But I couldn't spot any. It looked like a normal Emery pic.

Jealousy burned in my body. I wanted pics from a weekend with my dad too. *Stop thinking about it,* I told myself. *If you go there again, you're going to get upset.*

Plus, Vivi and Thea were giving me absolutely everything I could want this weekend and more. And Dad *was* coming tomorrow. Even if I had to share him.

Taking a deep breath, I rolled my shoulders and tried, for the moment, to let it go. Wait. Before I closed Insta, I typed in a name.

Mila Bloom.

And there she was! Mila, grinning at the camera, had her face squished against Circe's in her profile pic. My finger hovered over her profile, too afraid to even tap on her name. It wasn't like Mila would know! But still!

Thea and Vivi came back, arms full of snacks and sodas, and deposited them on Vivi's bed.

"What're you doing?" Vivi asked. "You're very smiley!"

"Maybe looking for Mila on Insta. You know, just to *see.*"

Thea and Vivi hurried to sit beside me, and both stared at my phone.

"Oh, she's so cute!" Vivi said. "You two were right."

"Told you," Thea said.

"Are you going to click on her profile or just stare at that one pic?" Vivi asked, elbowing me.

"I'm scared! What if I hit the heart button accidentally? Then she'll know I was looking! Or what if I accidentally click 'follow'?"

"Then you'll . . . follow her," Thea said.

"Thea! She'll think I'm stalking her or something."

"No, she won't," Vivi said. "She'll be like, 'Cool, this girl I just met is checking out my pics. How nice!'"

"No way. I'll click very, very carefully on her profile." I managed a deep breath through my nose. "But I am *not* following her!"

Not yet, anyway.

Together, Vivi, Thea, and I looked through a few of Mila's pics. Most of them were adorable candids with Circe. From the way Mila looked at her, it was clear the mare meant everything to her. Just like Beau did to me.

"Look at that one!" Thea said, pointing to the screen. "It says Theodore Haven Middle School. She must go there."

"Where is that?" I asked.

My friends shrugged. A quick Google search told us it was just a few miles away.

"No pics of her with a girlfriend or boyfriend," Vivi said, nudging my arm. "That's a good sign."

I couldn't stop scrolling. In every photo, Mila had this smile. This really cute smile that lit up her entire face. It sounded like such a cliché, but it was true. I couldn't help but wonder what it might feel like to make her smile at me like that.

After we finished the movie, Thea pulled out a deck of tarot cards—reading them was one of her favorite hobbies.

"Those are so pretty," I said, looking at the pink cards with white ink. "Are they new?"

"Yup! I got them last week. I saw them online, and I couldn't resist." Thea brought the deck to her chest, hugging the cards. "Let's hope we get good energy tonight! Who wants to go first?"

"I do!" Vivi said. "This is so cool. I've never had anyone do this before."

"Thea's really good," I said, taking a nibble of extra-sharp cheddar cheese.

Vivi and I watched as Thea carefully shuffled the deck. She held the cards in her hand, almost as if weighing them.

"They're still not cleared," she said. "I need to shuffle again." She shuffled the cards, cut the deck in thirds, and then shuffled once more. "Okay, Vivi. What would you like to ask the cards? Think about something in your life that you'd like clarity about."

"So they're not like a Magic 8 Ball, right?" Vivi asked.

Thea smiled. "Right. Instead of a simple yes-or-no question, ask the cards something that requires more insight. It can be about love, life, school—anything! I'm going to pull one card for each of us."

Vivi tilted her head, thinking. "Ooh. Okay, I've got one."

Thea put the deck facedown in front of us, nodding. "Go ahead."

"What will happen if I date Asher?" Vivi put her hands on her cheeks. "I have to know!"

"All right, let's see." Thea took the top card off the deck and turned it faceup in front of her lap. "Ohhhh! You got an Ace of Cups!"

We all peered down at the card—one with an overflowing chalice.

"Is that good?" Vivi asked, looking from the card to Thea. "I don't know what that means!"

"It's very, very good," Thea said. "The Ace of Cups means you should feel safe in your relationship. Or the relationship you wish to embark upon. This card means you should look for the good in the other person because you're sure to find it!"

Vivi grinned. "I knew it! Asher's a good guy."

"The card also wants you to explore getting to know each other," Thea said, "and look for the potential in Asher. It will open you up to becoming an even better person if you go into a relationship looking for the best in your partner."

"Basically, you should marry him," I teased. "He sounds perfect! This is so exciting."

Vivi laughed. "Maybe one day! But for now, we need to go on a date first."

"Fiiine, I guess that'll work," I said, tipping my chin to Thea. "You should go next. I'm still thinking of my question."

She shuffled the deck again before placing it in front of

her. "What should I do"—she paused, looking at Vivi and me—"to make my friendships last forever?"

"Aw," Vivi and I said together.

"You don't need cards for that," I said. "Just keep doing exactly what you're already doing."

Thea smiled. "Still. Let's see what they say!" She turned over the top card, smiling when she saw it.

"Knight of Swords," I read. "He looks cool, and I don't even know what the card means."

On the pink card, a knight was atop a horse, thrusting his sword into the air.

"Well, I was looking to him for advice," Thea said, "and I got it. This card means I need to surround myself with people who challenge me and who aren't 'yes' people."

"Meaning people who won't call you on it if you're out of line?" Vivi asked.

Thea nodded. "Yeah, I think so. It's telling me to keep the lines of communication open and to be clear when I do talk to my friends."

"That's solid advice for all of us," I said.

"It makes me think of Selly and Nina," Vivi said. "Their

relationship is super toxic. Nina never, ever calls Selly out on anything and vice versa. They let each other be mean, awful humans, and neither ever goes, 'Hey, you think this is a bad idea? Maybe we shouldn't do it.'"

"I'd be mad at you both if you always told me all my ideas were great and didn't tell me no or talk me out of stuff if you knew it was a bad plan," I said. "That's what being a *good* friend is."

"For sure." Thea nodded, picking up a peach ring and taking a bite. "Friends are supposed to support you and tell you when you're about to make the wrong decision. But I agree with Vivi. I don't think that's how it works between Nina and Selly at all."

"Or," I said, grimacing, "they're both so equally terrible that they really do love each other's bad ideas. Like, maybe Nina cheers Selly on when she's super rude to me. Or they talk about how best to rattle Thea and me in the arena."

"If I'm ever that awful," Vivi said, glancing at Thea and me, "you two better tell me. And turn me around."

Thea and I promised we would.

"Do you think the way Nina's changed has anything to do with her parents' divorce?" Thea asked.

I frowned. "I didn't hear anything about that."

"I only heard bits and pieces at the stable," Thea said. "But maybe it has something to do with how she's acting."

"Maybe," Vivi said.

I shrugged as Thea picked up the deck of cards. "Ready, Abs?"

Written in the Cards

I THINK SO," I SAID. "I'M NOT SURE IF IT'S a good question or not, but I have one."

Thea cut the cards, then shuffled the deck once more. "Okay. Ask away. The cards are cleared and ready."

"How will things be going by Halloween?" I asked. "I could use another good card!" I crossed my fingers, thinking of the card Thea had pulled for me before the show.

"Ooh, a question about the future," Thea said, hand hovering over the deck. "I like it."

She flipped over the top card, and I leaned closer to look

at it. It was a Three of Swords, and there were three swords jabbed through a heart.

"Hmm," Thea said.

I sucked in a breath. "Uh-oh. That sounds bad. You're not smiling, and you said, 'Hmm.' What does that card mean?"

"Ah, well," Thea started. "It means . . . you know. Things."

"*Thea.*"

"Things that maybe sometimes aren't great," she said. "But these cards can be silly. It's just for fun, anyway!"

"Tell me. What does it mean?" I locked eyes with her. "Just say it."

Thea sighed. "It means sadness, heartbreak, and betrayal. This card represents a warning sign, and it's a good idea to prepare yourself."

I sat in stunned silence. "Prepare for what?"

"I don't know," Thea said. "Abby, seriously, though, I'm not an expert at these cards. I could have drawn any one. It's not a science or anything."

"But you didn't. You drew that one."

She picked up the card and shuffled it back into the deck. "We could have a redo! Ask a new question. Or just draw another card."

"No," I said. "It's okay. Really. I got the Three of Swords. At least I got a warning for whatever is coming, I guess?"

Thea and Vivi gave me the same sympathetic smile.

"Whatever it is, if it's even anything, you'll get through it," Thea said.

"And we'll be right here," Vivi added.

"What if it's warning me about Mila?" I asked. "What if the card's saying not to ask her out or I'll be heartbroken?"

"No way." Thea shook her head. "I have a good feeling about Mila and her energy. I really, really don't think the card has anything to do with her."

I nodded, trying not to look as worried as I felt. I wasn't sure if I believed in tarot readings or not, but I couldn't help but feel unsettled by the card Thea had drawn for me. When she had drawn a good card for me, I'd clung to it as if I were sure it was the real deal. It didn't seem fair for me to pick and choose when I believed in the cards and when I didn't. But I didn't know how much more bad news I could handle. Not right now.

Vivi picked up her phone. "While we're all here, and I'm feeling brave, I'm going to do it. I'm going to text Asher and ask if he wants to go to the harvest dance with me."

"Yes, yes, do it!" I said.

"You're so brave," Thea said. "I could never!"

Vivi waved a hand. "Yes, you could! He's just a boy. And the worst that can happen is he'll say no, right?"

I grimaced. "Yes, but isn't that an awful and horrible possibility?"

"It would suck, but it's not *that* big of a deal to me," Vivi said. "If he says no, then I'll go with you two and have a great time." She looked back down at her phone. "Okay, here's what I'm sending. 'Hey! Hope you're having a good weekend. I wanted to ask if you'd like to go to the harvest dance with me. No pressure! Either way, I'll see you there.'"

My mouth fell open a little. "How did you do that? That's the best asking-someone-out text ever, and you sat here and came up with it in, like, seconds!"

"Please, teach me your ways," Thea said. "Seriously, that's a great text, Vivi. And the no-pressure part is my favorite. That's so smart, too."

"Thanks!" Vivi smiled. "I'm going to send it." Her thumb hovered over her phone, then she pressed the arrow. "Sent! Ahh!"

She tossed the phone toward the far end of the pile of blankets, laughing. "I'm not looking at it for a while. He could be busy too. I doubt he'll text me back right away and—"

Buzz!

Vivi's phone vibrated, making us all scream.

"Oh my god!" I said, laughing.

"It's got to be him!" Thea said. "Check it! Check it!"

Vivi shook her head. "Nooo! Now I'm all nervous!"

"What? No, why?" I half yelled. "You were fine—better than fine—when you sent it!"

"I don't know! I'm scared now! If it's Asher, he replied so fast. So, it's probably a 'thanks, but I'm good' text." She covered her face with her hands. "Someone else check."

"I will," Thea said, grabbing Vivi's phone. She leaned over so I could see the screen, and we tapped it awake.

Asher: That would be great. :) It's a date! (Haha, didn't mean to rhyme)

Thea and I grinned at each other as Vivi lowered her hands from her face.

"Well?" she asked.

"HE SAID YES!" Thea and I yelled at the same time.

"No way! He did?!"

Thea handed Vivi her phone, and a slow smile spread across her face to match ours.

"See?" I asked. "He even said, 'It's a date!'"

"Omigod." Vivi stared at her screen. "He did! I have a *date* to the harvest dance!"

She hugged her phone to her chest before flopping onto her back and staring at the ceiling.

I caught Thea's eye, and we laughed as we copied Vivi and lay back on the blankets.

Vivi covered her face with a pillow. "I can't believe it." Her voice was all muffled. "This is going to be awesome! And then we can start planning for the Halloween party!"

I crossed my fingers, hoping she was right and that the curse of my most recent tarot card wouldn't haunt me anytime soon.

"Team" Meeting

THE NEXT MORNING THEA TEXTED ME and Nina and asked us to meet her under the big oak tree by arena C. It was our final leg of the three-day event! As I headed that way, *definitely* not keeping my eyes peeled for Mila, I passed the other team of three—Keir, Selly, and Emery—as they were huddled together by one of the round pens.

Emery spotted me, and the look on her face was pure misery. She looked tired—dark circles visible under her eyes—and as if she'd rather be anywhere else.

Good. That was fine with me. I couldn't help but feel a

little satisfied with how unhappy she looked. Maybe she felt guilty for what she'd done. Or maybe hanging out with Selly and Nina wasn't as fantastic as she'd thought it would be.

She half raised her hand in a small wave, but I didn't return the gesture. Tonight's dinner with her was going to be plenty of face time.

As I hurried away from them, I thanked my lucky stars again for how Rebecca had split our teams. Keir was the captain of Emery's team with Selly, and Thea was the captain of my team with Nina. It could have been so much worse. As much as I hated having Nina on my team, at least she wasn't Emery. I shuddered a little, thinking about how bad it would be if I'd been stuck on a team with Nina and Selly. Or Nina and Emery. Or Emery and Selly.

Thea and Nina were already waiting under the tree. Nina's cropped brown hair was slicked back this morning, and she sipped a steaming thermos of something while Thea was on her phone. They both looked up as I approached.

Play it cool, I reminded myself. Nina didn't know that Emery had tipped me off to her being the Truth X. Poser. I still didn't know what I wanted to do with that, but I knew I'd have to confront Nina. One day.

I sneaked a glance at her, watching her nonchalantly sip her drink and look like everything was just fine and she hadn't been sending me harassing texts and emails and breaking into my room. But I didn't want to cause a scene, especially not at the start of our final phase of the competition.

"Thanks for coming," Thea said to me and Nina.

Like me, Thea was dressed in old breeches and an equally well-worn T-shirt. We knew not to wear our show clothes until right before it was our turn. The last time I'd gotten dressed early, Beau had wiped his grassy mouth on my white shirt after I'd let him take a few bites before getting him fully tacked up.

I'd been forced to hand him off to Thea, run back to the tack room, and find my emergency shirt that I kept just in case. We'd almost been late because it had taken me those few extra minutes to change.

"I'm only here because I have to be," Nina said. "Or you'd no doubt tell Rebecca that I didn't show up, and she'd be angry that I wasn't being a good teammate."

"Awesome," Thea said flatly. "I'm so glad that's your main motivation for coming to a team meeting."

Nina shrugged. "It's a waste of time. I already know what to do."

"You know what?" Thea snapped, turning to her. "Go. Just go. If you're going to act like it's beneath you to be here, then you're wasting my time. I'll just tell Rebecca that you didn't want to be here."

"You wouldn't."

"Try me."

Nina gave an exaggerated sigh, blowing out a long breath. "Fine, whatever. What's the meeting about?"

Thea tipped her head in the direction of the round pen. "Them. Their team is right there with us score-wise for this show. I'm in the lead for our team, then Abby, then you."

"So, that means we're in good shape going into cross-country," Nina said. "Perfect."

"Only if we concentrate," Thea said.

Nina nodded. "I'm focused."

"We have to be a team," Thea said. "It's not just about you. We *all* have to be focused on good rides."

"Agreed," I said.

"Okay, so, any questions or thoughts or whatever about the course?" Thea asked. She held out her phone, tilting it sideways to look at the course map.

Nina and I peered at her screen.

After a moment, Nina said, "No. I don't think so. It seems pretty straightforward. We all need to come away with no faults."

"We're not going to have an easy time against the other Foxbury team," I said. "And that's not even taking into account everyone else from other stables."

"Yeaaah, ugh," Nina said. "Oh, speaking of everyone else, I watched one of Olivia Woolsworth's Instagram stories, and she was talking—and by 'talking,' I mean bragging—that she's been training all summer with Canterwood's new instructor from Germany. Some hotshot Olympic coach who is a gold-medalist eventer."

I frowned. "Great. It's going to be fun going up against her and Ava soon."

The two superstar equestrians from Canterwood Crest Academy were the last thing I'd needed at this show. They'd be at later ones, for sure, but for the first comp of the season, they'd stuck a little closer to home in Connecticut. Still, Canterwood Crest wasn't too far from Foxbury, and since we'd all be traveling for shows over the season, it was only a matter of time before we'd regularly face off against them.

"Speaking of competition," Thea said, "I did see Keir training the other morning. He and Magic looked good. I know he's typically at the bottom of our group in lessons, but . . ."

I nodded. "I noticed that too. He's been working really hard, and it shows."

This competition wasn't going to be easy. As much as I'd wanted it to be, as the first show of the season, everyone had stepped up their game over the summer. I felt as though I'd been the only one who had stayed home and tooled around in the arena on Beau. We hadn't done any hard-core practicing aside from solo sessions, and I was no Rebecca. So I was worried we weren't going to be up to par with everyone else.

Nina stood a little straighter, pushing her shoulders back. "They're good, yes. We know. But so are we."

"At least Ava and Olivia aren't here," I said, blowing out a breath.

"I'm glad they aren't here either," Nina said. "Olivia talks waaay too much."

Thea shrugged. "I'm still watching the recorded livestream of their show later, though."

"Same," Nina said. "I want to see if they got any better over the summer."

I winced. "Let's hope not."

It seemed as though Nina's prickly demeanor softened a little as we talked through our strategy and the different riders who might be hard to beat. And the more we talked, the more confident I felt about today. Our team was *ready*.

Thea checked her phone again. "So, we need to tack up, get into our show clothes, and get to the safety check in a little bit."

"I'll pass, no problem," Nina said.

"Me too," I said.

Thea nodded. "Good. Same here. Then we'll head over to the warm-up area and get ready. When I'm done, Rebecca has someone coming to grab Chaos to cool him out for me so I can check on you two before your rides and then cheer you on."

I couldn't help but smile. Thea was the best team captain. She wanted our team to succeed, and she was going above and beyond what was required to make sure Nina and I had the opportunity to do our very best, even if I couldn't stand looking in Nina's direction right now.

"That sounds good," I said. "Thanks for sticking around."

Thea smiled back. "Of course! This is our first show of the season, and I want us to get off on the right foot for the rest of the comps. Today's not going to be a slam dunk, I don't think, but we can do everything possible to stay even points-wise with Keir, Selly, and Emery."

"Staying even is good and all," I said, "but I want to win."

"Me too!" Nina said. "Forget staying even, Thea."

Thea snorted. "All right, then! I have zero problems with this. I was trying not to push extra pressure on us, but let's win!"

I looked over at Nina, trying to decide what to do. She was being chill now, and my fury had subsided while we'd talked through today. If I could keep it all in, hold it all together, I could confront her after the show. That would be so much better, obviously, for many reasons.

Thea cleared her throat, toeing some grass in front of her with her boot. "Before we go, I know there are some"—she paused—"*issues* with our team. But we have to be careful."

"Issues?" Nina asked. "Why?"

I snorted. "Gee, I wonder."

"Come on," Thea said. "We were having a perfectly nice chat!"

"Who says we still aren't?" Nina asked, smirking at me. "Do tell, Abby. Why are there *issues* on our team?"

I bit the inside of my cheek, wondering if Nina somehow sensed that I knew the truth: that she was the TXP.

I tried to tell myself to keep my mouth shut and let it go. Like always, Nina was clearly trying to get a rise out of me. But the smirk on her face, and how she'd gone from talking about the course to poking me to see what would happen, made me angry. And that was on top of the anger I'd been bottling up since I'd learned she was the TXP.

"Let's focus on the show, okay?" I asked.

"Yeah, let's not argue now," Thea said.

"Sure, sure," Nina said. She tipped her chin toward Thea. "We good to go?"

"Yeah, I think we've covered everything," Thea said.

Nina started to walk away but turned back to us. "You better be careful," she said, staring at me. "It can be dangerous to ride when you're shaking like that."

What?

I glanced down, realizing my hands were trembling at my sides. I closed my fists, trying to stop the shaking. But I was so angry at Nina.

Nina sauntered away toward the stable, and Thea sighed. "Abby, you have to talk to her."

"I'm trying to wait," I said. "I don't want to create any more drama here."

"I'm not saying you have to *yell* at her. But she's right. You're shaking. You're distracted and angry. Which I get! But it's not going to magically disappear when you get on the course."

"I know. Ugh." I scrubbed my forehead with my hand. "You know what? I'm going to talk to her. Right now. No yelling. Super calm."

Thea chewed on her bottom lip. "I think you have to. There's so much going on right now from Nina to Emery that anything you can settle this morning before you ride might help."

I had no idea how I'd get through this if not for Thea. She always, always looked out for me.

"Okay, I'm going to go talk to Nina. Cross your fingers for me!"

Thea held up her hand, fingers crossed, and with a wave, she started toward the other barn while I went in the direction I'd seen Nina go. As I walked, I practiced in my head what I wanted to say. I didn't want to fight with Nina, not today, but I needed to get everything out. If I didn't, Thea was right: it was only going to continue to build up, and it would affect me at every turn, especially when I was riding.

The stable yard teemed with students as they tacked up, talked strategy, and shined boots and saddles. Everyone here wanted to have a great start to the season, myself included.

I found Nina alone in the tack room, running a soft cloth over her already gleaming saddle.

"Look, I wasn't going to do this now, but we need to talk," I said.

Nina didn't even glance up. "Okay?"

Everything she'd done rushed back to me. From the horrible emails to the texts to defacing my whiteboard. I wanted her to look at me and apologize. I needed her to know that what she'd done wasn't remotely okay. But I had to do it in a way that didn't draw attention to us—not when there were so many people roaming around on show day.

"I know," I said simply, letting the words hang in the air.

Nina looked up, her gray-green eyes settling on mine. "You know what?"

I took a step closer to her. "I know what you did. I know it was you."

That wiped the smirk off her face. She struggled to regain her composure, putting down the cloth and folding her arms across her chest.

"You know what I did, huh? What exactly do you think I did?"

"Not *think*. Know. I know you're the Truth X. Poser."

Nina shrugged. "And?"

"*And?* That's it? You're not going to try and deny it?"

"Why? I'm betting Emery sold me out, right? There's no way you and your merry little band of besties figured it out."

"It doesn't matter, does it? You're not denying it."

I don't know why I even bothered trying to protect Emery, as if she were innocent in any of this. But it still didn't feel right to toss out her name. Not when Nina was going to be angry that her secret was out there.

She waved a hand. "I don't care if you know. In fact, I'm kind of touched that Emery finally ratted me out and told you. Like, aw. She wanted to protect her big sister."

That wasn't how it had gone down. At *all*. But I wasn't telling Nina that.

"Yup," I lied, trying to project an air of unity between Emery and me. "But enlighten me, seriously. Why did you do this?"

Nina snorted. "Do I need some deep dark reason?"

"Any reason would work. I'm just curious."

"Selly." Nina's jaw tightened. "You got her in trouble and messed up her chances at team captain."

Of course this was about Selly. I shook my head. If only Nina wanted to protect someone who actually cared about her and didn't collect people like dolls so she could manipulate them.

"That was an accident! How did you even find out?"

"Please," Nina said. "I'm not telling you everything."

"It doesn't matter." I tried to keep my voice from creeping up louder. "However you found out, you did. And like I told you, it was a mistake!"

"Like you just said, 'It doesn't matter.' What you did still hurt Selly, and if it weren't for you, she'd be captain now instead of Keir."

I felt the wave of guilt that I always felt whenever I thought about my mistake and what it had cost Selly.

"Nina, you and I were friends once. I think I was a pretty good friend to you. So that means you've had at least one person not be a total jerk to you, and you know what real, actual friendship is like. But you've changed so much." I paused. "Is everything okay?"

"'Everything'?"

"Like, at home?"

Nina's eyes widened. "What?"

"I heard that your parents—"

"Don't talk about my parents," Nina growled. "They have nothing to do with this." She swallowed hard.

"Okay, I won't, but can you talk to Selly if there *is* something going on? Can you talk to her at all? She treats you like crap. Worse than crap, honestly. When has she ever had your back?" I caught Nina's eye. "You care about her. That's obvious. You did all this because I hurt her, and while I kind of admire that in some weird, twisted way, you have to know she wouldn't do the same for you."

Nina was silent, but there was something about the look on her face that told me she knew I was right.

"Would she?" I asked, pressing her a bit more. "Would Selly go out of her way to do something—*anything*—for you?" I paused for a second. "I'm not trying to hurt you by saying any of that, Nina, even as angry as I am. But it's the truth, and you have to know that."

"You don't know anything about my friendship with Selly," she said. "Maybe she's not all warm and fuzzy, but she cares about me."

"Does she say it, or does she show it? Because those are two different things. She can say it all she wants, but if she's not showing it, those are just empty words."

She sniffed, drawing herself up taller. "Selly's a good friend. She didn't deserve what you did to her."

"You're right—she didn't. I should have told her," I said. "But I didn't, and this is between us. It has nothing to do with you."

"It has everything to do with me. I know. She doesn't."

"So what? You're going to tell her?"

"Not yet. Maybe not at all. That depends on you."

"You're blackmailing me? Again?" I snorted. "Forget it."

"Oh, no, I'm giving you a choice." Nina stepped closer to me, her eyes flashing in the tack-room light. "You tell anyone what I did to you, and I'll tell Selly *and* Rebecca what you did."

The mere thought of Selly finding out was enough to make me want to barf. But Rebecca, too? I couldn't even begin to process the idea of telling her that I'd covered my own mistake to keep myself out of trouble. Rebecca would never, ever trust me again.

"But—"

"If I go down, you're going with me," she interrupted.

"It'll be worth it to take you down. I'll tell Selly and Rebecca right now."

"Do it." She cracked a smile. "Go on."

I opened and closed my mouth, unsure what to say now. Nina had totally called my bluff, and she knew it. I'd blown it.

"Are you going to keep harassing me?" I asked.

She waved a hand. "No. Where would the fun be in that? You know who I am now."

"Yeah, major bummer that you can't violate my privacy in peace."

She grinned. "That was actually a little funny. I'm glad you know, honestly. Whew. Now I don't have to waste my time messaging you anymore."

"Wonderful."

We glared at each other.

"We all set, Abs?"

I ground my teeth together so hard, it was a miracle they didn't crack. "Totally."

"Super! See you in the arena."

And with that, Nina turned back around to her tack, whistling as she picked up the cloth and started cleaning again.

GLHF

A WHILE LATER, I TOOK A DEEP BREATH and walked Beau toward the start box. After my little chat with Nina, I'd gotten him ready and had managed to clear my mind. Cross-country, our favorite phase, was finally here, and that was what I needed to focus on.

"Good luck, Abby!" Rebecca said as she walked over. "You're going to do great. Keep him even and actively moving forward."

"Thanks! I will."

Nerves fluttered in my stomach. We had to crush this!

"Hey, Abby Obviously! Good luck!"

I almost gave myself whiplash as I twisted around to look in the direction of the voice. Mila smiled as she walked over toward Beau and me. She looked beyond adorable in breeches and a violet T-shirt with a faded Foxbury logo on it. Her hair was in double French braids, and if she'd done them herself, I was going to need her to teach me how.

"Th-thanks!" I said. "You too!"

Oh my god. I wanted to dig my heels into Beau's sides and gallop away. *You too?* Mila wasn't even riding today! Could I not have one convo with her without saying something stupid?

"I mean, thank you!" I said, my face burning from embarrassment.

Mila smiled, that dimple popping on her left cheek. "See you after!"

Then she and Rebecca headed toward one of the spectator points to watch, and I guided Beau into the start box.

See. You. After.

Mila was going to see *me* after. Me. Abby St. Clair.

"She's going to be watching, boy," I whispered to Beau. "Let's make this round the best ever!"

The bell sounded, and I turned Beau in a slow half circle and let him out of the start box at a trot. Once we were a few strides away, I asked him for a canter. A warm wind whipped my ponytail back, and excited chills went up and down my arms.

Beau snorted, tugging on the reins, and I let him out a hair as we cantered toward the first obstacle. I counted down strides, and at exactly the right second, Beau flew into the air and we soared over the brush jump. He landed cleanly on the other side, and I used my hands and seat to urge him forward and asked for a bit more speed. Beau responded and sped up as he cantered with ground-eating strides.

We reached a log fence, and Beau took it without hesitation. I slowed him as we cantered toward another brush jump. But this one had a ditch in front of it. I didn't want Beau to be spooked by the ditch and try to look down into the empty, open space, so I kept his head up and asked him to lengthen his stride. I remembered what Rebecca had said about forward riding, and I kept pressure on him with my legs and seat.

As we approached the jump, I kept my own gaze off the ground and looked ahead. Beau hesitated, thinking about what I was asking him to do, but I urged him forward. He listened and soared over the ditch and brush.

"Good job, boy!" I whispered to him.

Three down, four to go!

We hit a stretch of flat land, and I stood in the stirrups and asked Beau to gallop. This was part of the course where I could let him go and we could shave serious seconds off our time. Beau was totally and completely up for it—he lengthened his stride and quickened his pace.

I smiled as the thrill from galloping hit me. Nothing in the world could beat this feeling! We hurried over the grass, perfectly in sync with each other, and it wasn't long before the next jump came into view: a whitewashed fence with yellow tulips on both sides of the rail.

I slowed Beau to a canter, and as we approached, I started counting down strides.

Four, three, two, one, *now!*

Beau leaped into the air, his legs tucked under his body. We sailed over the fence and flowers and started up a hill toward the fifth jump.

We were making excellent time, and Beau was giving it everything he had. I was so proud! At the top of the hill, the ground leveled off, and I guided Beau over an oxer with a tarp on the ground in the middle.

We took our time coming down the hill, and when we hit

the flat ground again, I asked Beau for a fast canter.

"Two more to go, boy," I told him. "Let's finish this!"

Beau flicked an ear back, listening to me, then charged ahead. We soared over a tire jump and headed for the final obstacle—a faux stone wall.

You can do it, I told myself. One final jump to go!

Beau cantered for the center of the jump, and at the right second, I crouched into a two-point position as he propelled himself off the ground. It felt like flying! His entire body was in the air as we soared over the wall. He landed clean on the other side, and I gave him the rein he wanted to hurry over the finish line.

"Way to go, boy!" I said, easing him to a trot. "We did it!"

Beau pranced for a few strides, tossing his head and sending his mane everywhere. He was so proud too! We'd gone clean and hadn't accumulated any time penalties.

"Let's get you cooled down a bit and checked out," I said. "Then you deserve some carrots. Big ones."

I hopped off his back and loosened his girth. I couldn't wait to see how we'd placed! Together, we started toward the vet check, and I grinned when Mila headed in our direction.

"That last jump was pretty perfect," she said.

"Thank you! Beau did so great."

She patted his neck. "He did. So did you."

I felt warm from my toes to my ears.

"I have to get him checked out," I said. "Are you watching the next rider?"

Mila shrugged. "I was going to, but actually, I need to check Circe's water bucket. Cool if I wait for you to finish the vet check? Then we could walk back to the barn?"

"Oh, yeah, sure. It won't take long."

Be cool, Abby. Be cool.

"Sweet."

As I led Beau into the tent, I felt as though I were floating. Our ride combined with the fact that Mila had hung out and watched us? This was pretty far beyond perfect.

A while later, Nina, Thea, and I were gathered together as we waited for the final results to go live. We all had our phones out and were watching the local IPL website. Keir had just completed his cross-country round, and scores would go up any second. I refreshed the page and then—

"YESSSS!" Thea screeched.

Nina jumped up and down. "WE WON!"

NO	RIDER	HORSE		DRESS. SCORE	SHOW JUMPING JUMP FAULTS	TIME FAULTS	SJ TOTAL	CURRENT RIDING TOTAL	CRO JUMP FAULTS	ELAPS TIM
	TEAM NAME/STABLE		PLACE: 1						RIDING SCORES	
	TEAM 2/FOXBURY									
17	THEA SONG*	CHAOS GREMLIN		31.00	0.00	0.00	0.00	31.00	0.00	3.2
23	ABIGAIL ST. CLAIR	BEAU OF MINE		32.83	4.00	0.00	4.00	36.83	0.00	3.1
28	NINA WILKERSON	ADORE		32.00	8.00	0.00	8.00	40.00	0.00	3.1
				BEST 3			BEST 3			
	*DENOTES TEAM CAPTAIN		TEAM TOTALS	95.83			12	107.83		

"Our team snagged first, and Thea, you won overall!" I said. "Way to go!"

And there was my name in *second* place!

Keir, Selly, and Emery had come in second place as a team, and Emery had snagged sixth place overall.

"We did it, team!" Thea said, high-fiving me and then Nina.

"First show of the season, and it's a win for us," Nina said. "I'm really, really excited to start off with those points."

"Regionals, here we come!" I said.

"Let's go get our ribbons," Thea said.

Together, as a team, the three of us hurried toward the judges' tent to claim our prizes. I felt as though I'd never stop

JLTS	XC TOTAL	RIDING TOTAL	SETUP SAFETY	REQ. EQUIP	TURN OUT	DAY 1	DAY 2	DAY 3	XC	MISC HM	HM SCORE	TOTAL SCORE
						HORSE MANAGEMENT SCORES					TOTALS	
0.00	0.00	31.00	0.00	0.00	0.00	0.00	0.00	0.00			0.00	31.00
0.00	0.00	36.83	0.00	0.00	0.00	0.00	0.00	0.00			0.00	36.83
0.00	0.00	40.00	0.00	0.00	0.00	0.00	0.00	0.00			0.00	40.00
	BEST 3		0.00	0.00		0.00		0.00			0.00	0.00
	0	107.83	0.00	0.00	0.00			0.00	0.00	0.00	0.00	107.83

smiling. One show was down, and I was one step closer toward redeeming myself from last season and getting to regionals. Then? Nationals.

Beau and I were going all the way this year, and nothing was going to stop us!

My Main Course: A Hockey Puck

L ATER THAT EVENING, I WENT TO THE
parking lot to meet the Uber that Dad and Natalie
had sent for me and Emery. I stood in the parking
lot, arms folded, as Emery walked over to me. She was dressed
up a little for dinner, like I was, in a cute green dress and flats.

"Hey," she said.

"Hi."

We stood there in silence as Emery played with the ends
of her hair.

"I thought you'd be with your mom," I said. "I was surprised when my dad told me you were grabbing the Uber too."

Emery nodded, and I could see a bit of hope on her face that I was talking to her. "I came back for a while to get ready for school tomorrow. Plus, she wanted to go antiquing, and that's not really my thing."

"Gotcha."

"Abby, look," Emery said. "I know you don't want to talk to me. I get it. But please. Will you at least let me explain?"

"No. No, Emery, I won't." I took a breath. "I meant what I said yesterday. I don't want to talk about it. I don't want to hear you out. The only thing I do want? Is for my dad not to know there's a problem between us. Can you at least do that?"

Her nose twitched as her eyes filled with tears. But she fought to keep any from falling and nodded. "Yeah. Whatever you want."

"Thanks."

We didn't speak for the entire ride. We got out of the Uber, and my dad and Natalie stood together near the restaurant entrance, waiting for us. We said our hellos, and I even hugged Natalie.

"It's so good to see you both!" Dad said as we took our seats at the table he'd reserved.

"You too," Emery said, smiling at him.

"It smells amazing in here," I said. "I can't wait to eat!"

My mission to make everything seem fine and normal was *on*. I did not want Dad or Natalie to pick up on anything with me and Emery.

The steak house dining room was beautiful, with dark wooden beams stretching across the ceiling, crimson-colored seats, and pretty chandeliers hanging every few tables.

We ordered our drinks, and I couldn't help but stare at Natalie and Dad. They were seated across from me and Emery, and they kept shooting each other quick little glances, like all they wanted to do was hold hands. Or kiss. I shuddered. *Gross.*

"I'm still so proud of you both," Dad said. "Your first show back after summer break, and you both did so, so well."

"Thanks, Dad," I said. "Beau was really good, and he did everything I asked."

Emery nodded. "Bliss, too. I think she had a little too much fun on the cross-country course. But we'll work on it."

"Abby's cross-country round was spectacular," Natalie said, eyes a little wide. "I wish I'd gotten video of this one brush jump. It was so beautiful!"

"You were there?" I asked. I hadn't seen Natalie with any of the spectators, not that I'd been paying too close attention to them.

"Of course I was." She said it with such ease, as if I should have expected her and counted on her all along. I swallowed. Hard.

"I didn't see you," I said, "but I'm . . . I'm glad you were there."

It meant a lot to me, honestly. More than I could even let myself feel right now while I was at dinner with everyone.

Natalie took a sip of her water and then gave me a big smile. "Me too, Abby. It was fun watching you and Beau compete."

I looked over the menu, taking in all the options. "Steak for me tonight," I said. "Yum!"

The waiter came over to take our order. When it was my turn, Dad hung his head a little and glanced down at the table.

"Forgive my daughter for how she's about to order her steak," he murmured.

I laughed. "Sorryyy!" Then I looked at the waiter. "I'd like mine *beyond* well-done. Like, once the chef thinks it's done? Cook it past that."

"She wants a hockey puck, basically," Dad said with a sigh.

The waiter looked horrified by my request. "Let me write that down. 'Hockey puck.' Got it."

"Thank you!" I said sweetly.

Dad gulped his water in shame as the waiter told us he'd be back soon with our food and walked off.

"You really like your steak that way?" Emery asked, shaking her head.

"Yup," I snapped, unable to keep the attitude out of my tone.

Emery just nodded.

"I'm going to change the subject now," Dad said, "or I'll try to talk Abby into eating her steak differently. Again." He winked at me.

He didn't really care how I ate it. It was something he loved to tease me about, and I liked trying to rile him up over it.

"So, what's on your agendas for next week?" Natalie asked. "Besides school and riding, of course."

"There's a cross-country trial on Sunday," Emery said. "It'll be great practice for Bliss and me."

"You going, Abs?" Dad asked.

"Yup, definitely."

"That'll be fun," Natalie said. "I can't wait to hear how you two do."

"And there's the harvest dance on Friday," I said.

Dad sat up a little straighter and put his glasses on top of his head. "A dance, huh? Going with anyone? You haven't mentioned any crushes lately!"

"Daaad," I said.

Even though talking about crushes with my *father* wasn't something I wanted to do, I knew how lucky I was to be able to do it. Dad had been supportive of me from the moment last year when I'd told him I was queer—definitely liking girls and *maybe* liking boys. He'd even taken me to Boston Pride last summer, and we'd had a blast.

But he just grinned at me. "Any cute boys on your radar? Or any cute girls?"

Just Mila, I wanted to say. Instead, I said, "There *might* be a girl. And I'm not sure yet. Vivi and Thea will be there, though, so we'll be hanging out."

"Are you going, hon?" Natalie asked Emery.

She nodded. "Yeah! Zoe, Wren, and I are planning on

going together. I'm excited. I've never been to a dance like that before."

"You haven't?" I couldn't stop myself from asking.

"Nope." She shrugged. "I didn't really go to dances. Anything like that, really. I was too busy riding."

"Wow. I didn't know that."

It wasn't like Emery and I ever talked about that kind of stuff.

The waiter came with our plates, and when he set mine down in front of me, he grimaced. "Enjoy . . . *that*."

"I will!" I said brightly. "Thank you!"

I got ready to dig in, and then I noticed Dad, Emery, and Natalie eyeballing my plate.

"That's definitely a hockey puck," Natalie said.

All of us laughed, and for a moment, I sort of forgot that I hated Emery.

After I devoured my delicious hockey puck and everyone else had eaten their food, we had brownies and ice cream for dessert. Dad ordered our car back to Saddlehill, and he pulled me aside while Natalie told Emery about the treasures she'd found antiquing.

"It was really good to see you, Abs," Dad said, hugging me.

I squeezed him back. "Yeah, it was good. And thanks for coming. It meant a lot."

He gave me a sad smile. "I'm really sorry for missing the show. I know I already told you on the phone, but I wanted to apologize in person, too. I'm going to do better with keeping my word."

"I know you're sorry. And I'm sorry I lost it on you."

"It's understandable." He studied my face. "Is everything else okay? It feels like something's up."

After seeing how happy he'd been tonight, with Natalie and with Emery and me there together, there was no way I was telling him anything.

"Nope, everything's good! The show was stressful, so that's probably it."

"All right. But if there's something else that you want to talk about, you know I'm here for you, right?"

I nodded. "Thanks, Dad."

Our Uber came, and Emery and I said goodbye to our parents.

Once we were off in the direction of Saddlehill, I blinked hard, trying to stop tears from forming. I couldn't stop myself from wishing that Emery hadn't betrayed me with Nina. If she hadn't, that entire happy family dinner we'd just had would have been real. As real as I seemed to wish it had been.

"Abby?" Emery asked, her voice soft.

I sniffed, glancing from the window to her. "What?" There was more bite in my tone than I'd intended.

"Nothing." Emery looked away from me. "Never mind."

And we spent the rest of the ride in silence just like earlier. It didn't matter what I wished for. Emery had already blown up our relationship. There was no coming back from that.

Anxious Rambles

ON MONDAY I WENT TO THE STABLE and hung out with Beau in his stall after our lesson. I'd been giving myself a pep talk for the last fifteen minutes to psych myself up to ask Mila to the harvest dance.

"I'm gonna do it, boy," I whispered to him. "Right now. I got this."

But as I pulled myself out of his stall, I didn't at all feel like I had it. Puking or fainting didn't seem out of the question! And, like, this was only the beginning of asking people to dances and parties. I had to do this for the rest of my *life*! Unless, of course, people asked me.

Muttering under my breath the exact words I wanted to say, I headed down the aisle and spotted Mila outside Circe's stall. She reached up to hang the mare's halter on a hook and then spotted me.

"Hey!" she said, smiling.

I couldn't help but smile back. Hers always made me feel gooey inside. "Hi! All finished for today?"

Mila nodded. "Yup. Circe had a lot of energy today, so we did some work in the round pen."

"Did that wear her down a bit?"

"Big-time."

Mila lifted Circe's saddle off her tack trunk, and I grabbed the mare's bridle. Together, we walked toward the tack room, and I tried to breathe and not panic. *Do it, Abby. Ask her!*

But once we got inside, I busied myself hanging up Circle's bridle and cleaning the bit for Mila. Once it was beyond spotless, I turned to her and tried to ignore my heart beating out of my chest.

"So!" I said. "On Friday, did you hear?"

That was not at *all* what I'd planned to say. How was she supposed to have heard about things going on at Saddlehill? She didn't even go there!

"Hear what?" She stopped wiping Circe's saddle and looked at me.

"There's, um, something happening!"

"Oh yeah?" Mila asked. "Do tell!"

Her eyes had this *sparkle* in them, and for a few seconds, I forgot that she was waiting for me to speak. I wiped my slick palms on my breeches.

"It's going to rain!" I blurted out.

Oh my god. I wanted to fall through the floor, never to be seen again.

Mila tilted her head, frowning a little. "Rain? I didn't hear that."

"Lots of rain," I said. "Buckets. Actually, I have to go get ready for . . . *that*."

Before I rambled on for one more sentence about the fake weather forecast, I bolted from the tack room, nearly smacking into the doorjamb on my way out.

Major. Fail.

* * *

When Wednesday finally rolled around, I was so ready to get to the stable already. But first, I had to survive classes.

At lunch, I slid into my usual seat at the table near the window and put down my tray. Ankita and Willa were already chowing down on turkey subs.

"Guess what?" Willa asked me.

"What?" I asked.

"Last night, I asked a certain someone to the harvest dance!" she squealed, grinning.

"Omigod, Wills!"

"She said yes, obviously! Quinn and I are going together! I can't even!"

I smiled so hard, it made my cheeks hurt.

"You two are gonna be the cutest couple," I said. "This is so exciting!"

"They're going to be so adorable," Ankita said around a mouthful of sandwich.

This was a huge moment for Willa. She'd liked Quinn for so long, and even though I didn't really know Quinn, I'd seen some of the texts she'd sent Willa. She was funny, sweet, and quick to compliment Willa.

Vivi and Thea sat down, all smiles as Willa told them about Quinn.

"Hopefully," I said, crossing my fingers under the table, "I'm also going with someone."

"You're asking her today?!" Thea asked.

I nodded. "I have to! The dance is on Friday. I tried to ask Mila on Monday, but I got all awkward and weird and couldn't make myself do it."

"Oh nooo," Vivi said. "Well, you tried! Next time, you'll do it."

"What do I say?" I asked.

"Try something like, 'Hey, harvest dance at Saddlehill on Friday! Want to come?'" Thea said. "Quick. To the point."

"If I can actually get it out," I said.

"You can," Willa said. "Then we'll both have girls to dance with."

That made me smile. "Okay, okay. I can do this."

"She'll say yes, Abs," Vivi said. "Unless she really, truly already has plans that have nothing to do with her not wanting to go with you."

I groaned. "If I'd asked her earlier, she wouldn't have these hypothetical plans!"

"Let's talk about something else or you're going to keep worrying," Thea said. "What's everyone wearing?"

"Ooh," Willa said, pulling out her phone. "Look at this shirt I found."

I waited for her to open the shopping app, forcing myself to eat my yogurt and trying to stay in the moment, even though my head was already at the stable.

A few hours later, I climbed off the bus and started across the Foxbury campus toward the main barn. It was riding lesson day for us, and I had a feeling Mila would be here too. Or I hoped she would be, anyway.

The stable was fairly busy, with riders grooming and tacking up their horses. I sidestepped around a black gelding in crossties and made my way to Beau's stall.

"Hey, hey," I said to him when he poked his head over the stall door. "How're you doing?"

Beau pushed his head into my hands, and I scratched his forehead.

"Let's get you groomed, boy," I said. My eyes zoomed in on the snippets of grass and clover clinging to his mane. "It looks like you had a nice roll in the pasture earlier."

It didn't take long to get his halter and lead line on, and I grabbed our grooming kit before we started out of the stable.

You're taking the easy way out, I told myself. *Go find Mila.* But that sounded scary!

"If you find her," I whispered to myself, "you actually have to talk to her! What if she says no? Or what if she laughs at you?"

"Who's going to laugh at you?"

I jumped, halting Beau and turning to see Mila standing there, looking at me with a curious expression.

"Hi!" I said. "No one. Well, maybe someone. I mean, I hope not!"

"I hope this 'someone' doesn't. Or I'll be mad at them."

I laughed. "Thanks." I wanted to ask her. Right now! But the words didn't come out, and instead of asking her, I played with the end of Beau's lead rope. "Have you groomed Circe yet?"

"Nope, but I was planning on it." Mila reached over and patted Beau's shoulder. "Want company?"

"Sure!" It came out a little too loud.

"I'll grab Circe and meet you at the grooming posts by the trees."

All I could do was nod. Then, once she was safely out of sight, I squeezed Beau's neck in a quick hug and held myself back from squealing in his ear. I tried not to skip the entire way to the posts.

It wasn't long before Mila and Circe headed our way. Mila's grooming tote was purple, just like her shirt.

"Is purple your favorite color?" I asked as she tied up Circe next to Beau.

"Yeah! All shades of it, actually. I've bought Circe so much purple stuff, it's kind of ridiculous."

"Purple's pretty. It looks good against her gray coat."

"I think so too." Mila smiled. "What's your favorite color?"

"Teal. I'm with you on buying too much stuff—I have lots of halters, leads, blankets, everything in as much teal as I can find."

"I love teal! I wore a teal dress to a party last year." She dug around in her grooming kit and held up her phone. "Want to see it?"

"Sure!" I walked over to her, standing close enough now that I could smell her body spray. Mila smelled like vanilla and strawberries. *Oh my god, Abby, don't be creepy!* I focused my attention on her phone as she opened Instagram and scrolled to find the photo she wanted.

"Here it is," Mila said.

I looked closer at the screen to see a smiling Mila in what was in fact a very teal dress paired with black Converse sneakers.

"Cuuute!" I said. "That color looks great on you. Especially with your hair."

Mila smiled, and that dimple popped in her cheek. "Thanks! Are you on Insta? I bet you post great pics."

"Yeah, I am. And I don't know about 'great,' but it's fun." I tried to manage what I hoped was a cute smile back.

She giggled a little. "What's your handle? I'd like to see your pics. Unless it's private!"

Ohhh. I wanted to smack myself in the face.

"Sorry," I said. "I didn't realize that's why you asked me. It's AbbyyStClair. Two *y*'s. Totally not private."

"Cool!" Mila tapped in my name, and a few seconds later, my phone dinged from my grooming kit. "I'm following you."

I swiped my phone from my kit and followed her back.

"Mutuals now," I said.

She smiled at me and went back to grooming Circe. I tried not to brush the same spot over and over on Beau while I thought of a way to ask Mila to come to the harvest dance.

We worked hard on our horses as we got them ready to ride.

"They seem to like each other already," Mila said. "That's so cute!"

Beau had reached his muzzle out to Circe, and the horses sniffed each other, letting out little grunts.

"Aww, they're being adorable! Do you have a lesson today?"

Mila nodded. "Yup. With Allie. She's helping me get ready to try out for the middle novice team."

"That's exciting. Allie's great, and she'll make sure you're ready to go for tryouts. You said they're soon?"

"Within the next few weeks. I hope we're ready by then."

"If you, you know, ever want to ride together and practice, we could," I said. "Although I'm sure you're practicing plenty with Allie."

"No—I mean, I'm getting plenty of hours in with her, but I'd love to ride with someone already on the team."

I ducked my head, trying to hide my blush. "It's a plan then."

Okay, okay, okay. *Just ask her,* I yelled at myself. I stepped around Beau to grab a soft cloth out of his grooming kit and stood by his head. "So, speaking of plans"—I wiped around Beau's eyes—"there's a thing at my school on Friday. A dance. A harvest dance! With fun stuff."

Mila peered around Circe to look at me. "Oh yeah? A harvest dance with fun stuff sounds cool."

"Right? I'm going!"

She smiled, a look in her eye like I was amusing her. "I figured."

"Do you"—I tried not to squeak out the rest of the words, but it seemed impossible—"want to go?"

"With you?"

"Yes, yeah, with me." I thought I was going to faint. If she said no, I'd surely crumble into the dirt.

"That would be great!" She dug her phone out of her pocket and placed it in my very, very sweaty palm. "Put your number in. Then you can text me details later."

Oh my god! *Don't faint, Abby.*

"Okay. Awesome!" My thumbs shook, and I pressed all the wrong numbers before finally getting the correct digits in her phone. "There." I handed Mila her phone back.

We went back to grooming our horses, and when I was sure she wasn't looking, I did a silent, ridiculous victory dance. I was going to the harvest dance with Mila!

Fall-ing for You

FRIDAY EVENING GOT HERE BEFORE I knew it, and I was running purely on panic. No caffeine necessary. In the spirit of trying to help me stay calm, Vivi had lit a lavender candle on her bedside table. So far, it wasn't doing much for my nerves, and I wasn't sold on the scent.

"It's cool enough today that I can wear flannel!" I told Vivi. "Is that dressy enough?"

"Totally. It's a harvest dance! Wear it open, with a T-shirt underneath and with dark-wash jeans." She said this all as if she needed zero time to think about it.

"And boots?" I asked.

"And boots," she confirmed.

I had a bunch of flannel shirts in my closet, but I knew the one I wanted: the purple-and-white one. Last night, I'd even painted my nails purple. Overboard? Probably.

I got dressed and looked over at Vivi. She'd paired a cozy burnt-orange sweater with jeans. "You look so cute!"

"Thanks!" she said, smiling at me. "It feels very fall to me without going full-on pumpkin territory."

"Save that for the Halloween bash."

"Exactly!"

"Are you as nervous about seeing Asher as I am about seeing Mila?" I asked.

Vivi stared in the mirror, concentrating on making her space buns even. "I don't think it's possible to be as nervous as you, but I'm kinda anxious. I know I hung out with him at the welcome-back party, but this feels different."

"Maybe because it's your second date? And now, you know you really like him so you want it to go well."

Vivi raised an eyebrow at me. "I bet you're right. I hope he likes me as much as I like him."

"Who wouldn't like you?" I came over to stand beside her

in front of our full-length mirror. "He better be great to you, or I'll hunt him down."

That made Vivi laugh. "Oh, you will now, huh?"

"Yup. It's best-friend code."

"Then the same goes for Mila. She better be great to you or *else*."

"Noted."

Vivi and I smiled at each other in the mirror.

"Ready?" she asked me.

"Not even a little bit!"

"Abs, you're going to have so much fun. Mila's so freaking lucky to be going with you, and don't forget that. And if things get awkward or weird, I'll be around. And so will Thea. And everyone else." She turned to me and put her hands on my shoulders. "It's going to be great!"

My mouth was dry, and I felt a little dizzy, but I nodded. "Okay. Let's go."

Together, Vivi and I left Amherst House and headed for the sports fields. The sun was starting to set, and the lights were popping on all over campus. The older students and some teachers had been working hard on decorating and setting up this week. I'd seen a hint of it when I'd jogged by the fields for gym. But I hadn't wanted to look more closely until it was finished.

My phone buzzed, and I almost dropped it. What if it was Mila saying she wasn't coming? I forced myself to check with one eye closed.

Mila: On campus! Be at the parking lot in a min :)

I showed my phone to Vivi.

"Yay!" she said. "I'm supposed to meet Asher at the caramel-apple booth."

"That sounds delicious."

"Right? Definitely take Mila there."

We went up a little hill and reached the sports-field parking lot. It was a warm evening with zero percent chance of rain, so we'd lucked out.

"*Whoa,*" I said, craning my neck to see more. "It looks amazing even from here!"

The iron fence between the parking lot and the field had been wrapped in brilliant orange-and-yellow leafy garland. Giant pumpkins sat on hay bales on either side of the entrance, and the entire field was full of activities, games, and food. Across the field, the gym was all lit up and ready for dancing. The smell of fried deliciousness wafted through the air, and I inhaled deeply.

"Do you want me to wait here with you for Mila?" Vivi asked. "Or are you okay?"

"Go! I'm good." Or I was pretending to be, anyway.

Vivi smiled. "Okay, see you in there."

She headed onto the field, and my heart pounded when a car pulled up. A very smiley Mila hopped out and waved at me.

Oh. My. God.

She looked *so* effortlessly cute! Her hair was down, flowing around her shoulders in soft waves. And she'd put a lilac cardi over a tee, which was tucked into her jeans.

"Hey!" Mila said.

"Hi!"

Don't be awkward, don't be awkward, I told myself.

Her eyes caught on my shirt. "That's such a great shirt."

"Thanks!" I waved one of my hands, in a *what, this old thing?* gesture. I nodded toward the field. "Are you ready?"

Mila grinned. "So ready. Something smells really good, and we have to find out what it is."

"Right? Let's go."

We walked to the field, and with every step, my anxiety began to ease. Mila seemed genuinely excited to be here . . . with *me.*

"Wow," she said, glancing around. "Now this is a harvest dance!"

The field was dotted with booths, from donuts to hot apple cider to pumpkin spice lattes. There were carnival games and an old-fashioned claw machine with stuffed animals inside. Lights were strung everywhere, and there was a giant standing map of where to find what activity.

"What do you want to do first?" I asked.

"Hmm," Mila said, peering at the map. "I don't know! There's so much."

"Maybe we wander around and see what we find?"

She turned toward me, smiling. "That sounds perfect."

Side by side, we strolled down the field. There were students everywhere, and it was fun to see Saddlehill teachers behind some of the booths.

"That's my art teacher," I said to Mila as I waved at Ms. Foster. She was overseeing a beanbag toss. "She's the best."

"Do you like art?" Mila asked.

"I do! It's a newer thing of mine. I love doodling Beau. Especially when I'm in math class and am supposed to be learning."

"Math is my favorite!" Mila said. "How dare you not pay

attention?" She laughed. "I'm that way with history. I would rather do anything else but try to memorize dates and battles and wars."

"Totally understand that. I like history, but the dates are something I could do without."

We reached a sign, and at the same second, we both turned to each other. Mila's eyes were wide.

"Hay-bale maze!" we said in unison.

We cracked up and dashed through the entrance. Rows and rows of hay bales were stacked higher than our heads in an intricate maze.

"This is going to be *fun*," I said. "Think we can find our way out?"

Mila nodded and stood a little taller. "Of course we can! I bet we figure it out in no time."

We looked right, left, then right again.

"Hmm," I said, "Maybe the exit's this way!"

"You think? I don't know, it feels too obvious. It's going to be a dead end."

"Want to bet?" I asked.

"You're on!"

Mila followed on my heels as we took a sharp right then a

left and . . . hit a dead end. A scarecrow mocked us, well, *me* for my mistake.

"Ha!" Mila said, sticking out her tongue playfully. "I win! I'll think about the terms of my payment later."

I laughed. "Fiiine. I'll follow you this time."

Mila reached for me and gently grabbed my wrist, tugging me forward. "This way!"

Even though the temperature was in the low seventies, a chill went up and down my arms. Mila was touching my wrist. I repeat: a cute girl was touching me! Why weren't Vivi and Thea here to see this?!

"You better be right, Bloom," I said, trying to sound chill, "or I get to pick the direction next!"

We wove through the hay bales, twisting and turning and definitely not getting any closer to the exit. But we were laughing and having so much fun that I didn't mind getting lost with Mila.

After a million wrong turns, we finally made it out of the maze. Mila and I grabbed glazed donuts and apple ciders. We played a few carnival games, and Mila kicked my butt in ring toss. Like, in an *epic* fashion.

"You didn't miss one!" I said, shaking my head. "Did I get bamboozled? I feel like I did."

She laughed. "*Bamboozled?* How?"

"You challenged me to ring toss but didn't tell me that you're some kind of champion at it. You have to be!"

"Well, I have a roomful of ring toss trophies at home. . . ." She caught my eye, giggling. "Just kidding! I got very lucky, that's all."

"Hmm," I mused as we walked shoulder to shoulder.

"Maybe I didn't want to look bad in front of you."

"Because you were afraid I'd never talk to you again if you sucked at ring toss? Accurate. Dang."

"I knew it." Mila shook her head, feigning despair.

We laughed. Being around her was easy. It felt like I'd known her forever but also like we'd just met moments ago. It was a weird combo, but I didn't know how else to explain it.

"Do you want to check out the gym?" I asked. "My friends might be there, and I could introduce you."

"That would be great." Mila smiled. "But you can just ask me, you know."

I looked at her sideways. "Ask you what?"

"To dance."

"Oh! Well, I wanted to. But I wasn't sure if you did. Then I got all weird and shy and—"

"You don't have to be weird or shy around me. But I also get it. I mean . . . I feel the same way around you."

"You do?"

She nodded. "Yeah."

We smiled at each other.

"Tonight's been really great," I said. "I'm so glad you could come!"

"Me too! I'm usually chilling in my room a lot on the weekend, so it felt good to go out and do something for once."

"Are you an introvert, or do you just like to stay in?"

"Hmm, I don't think I'm an introvert, exactly, but I do like to be in cozy clothes and watching TV and having snacks. Kind of a way to unwind after a hard week of classes and riding."

"I'm here for all the Netflix and snacking. Especially the snacking."

Mila raised an eyebrow. "Sweet or savory?"

"Savory! Salty stuff. Chips, crackers, cheese."

She raised a hand for me to high-five. "Same! All my friends are, like, sugar fiends. But I *crave* salt." Mila tilted her head. "You should come to my house sometime. If you want," she added quickly. "My mom shops at this fancy grocery store once in a while and gets the *best* cheeses. That's my prize! I want you to come over."

"Yum! And that would be so fun. Ever since I started going to Saddlehill, I don't get to go over to friends' houses much. Most of the people I know go here, so we just walk across campus to visit each other."

"That's so cool, though. I have a few friends who go to boarding schools, but this is the first time I've been here. Sometimes I wish I lived away from home! My parents are super concerned with my grades and extracurriculars and stuff, but I have other friends whose parents just let everything slide." She took a breath. "I know it's because they care, but it can be a *lot* sometimes."

I nodded as we strolled toward the gym. "It's kind of the opposite with my dad. He loves me a lot, and I know he does, but he's always busy with work. It's gotten worse over the years since my mom left."

Mila frowned. "I'm sorry, Abby. That's not fair."

"I'm used to it, I guess. Mostly. But he remarried over the summer, and I got a new stepsister, Emery. She's on the riding team, so you'll meet her. She's a year younger than us, with a mare named Bliss."

"Is she blond, and is Bliss a chestnut?" Mila asked.

"Yup and yup."

"I saw her around, then." Mila looked at me. "Is she a good stepsister?"

I drew in a breath. "She was at first. But then she did something that really hurt me." I shrugged. "I don't know if we'll get past it."

"That sucks. I hope you're able to, for your sake. I'm sure you'll have to spend time with her, so it would make things easier if you were able to talk it out."

"Definitely. We'll see. Things have been pretty busy with school and riding, but maybe we'll be able to work on it. Someday."

We reached the gym, and pop music flowed out of the open doors. Students were everywhere, and I tried to look confident about going inside, even if I was nervous about any potential dancing.

Together, we walked inside, and both of us stopped in our tracks to look around in awe.

"Wow," Mila said. "This looks fantastic!"

"Right?"

Everything was fall-themed: from the orange streamers to the earthy brown tablecloths to the orange, brown, and yellow balloons scattered all over the dance floor.

"Want to hit up the hot chocolate bar?" I asked Mila.

"Yes!"

The long banquet table was gorgeous. Faux leaves were everywhere, and someone had taken pumpkins, scooped out the guts, and filled the centers with vivid sunflowers and bright orange chrysanthemums. Tea lights set on top of candy-corn-filled jars looked so much like fall, it was ridiculous. Candles and copper-wire fairy lights were everywhere, casting warm light over the tables. There were so many decorative gourds too, and I had to reach out and touch one of them.

Down the table was a hot chocolate bar, complete with mason jars of options, from white chocolate chips to Hershey's Kisses to butterscotch chips.

I picked up a cup, filled it with hot chocolate, and handed it to Mila.

"Thank you!" Her eyes were bright as she smiled at me.

"No problem. Well, there *is* gonna be a problem, and that will be deciding what to put in my hot cocoa."

Mila laughed. "Oh, I couldn't agree more. But I think I'm going to go with dark chocolate chips and whipped cream."

"Yum!" Carefully, I surveyed my options. Again. "I think I'm going to go with butterscotch chips. No, white chocolate. No, butterscotch."

I went for it before I changed my mind and took the bowl of what looked like freshly made whipped cream from Mila when she held it out to me.

We moved away from the table, sipping our drinks.

"Oh, look!" I said, pointing to two girls on the dance floor. "That's my friend Willa and her date, Quinn."

Both girls bopped to the music, smiling at each other as they moved.

"Are they girlfriends?" Mila asked.

"Not yet, but I bet they will be soon. If not after tonight, then very soon. Aren't they cute together?"

Mila nodded, watching them. "Supercute!"

"Abs!"

"Hey!" I said, smiling at Vivi as she walked over to Mila and me. "Mila, this is my best friend, Vivi. Vivi, this is Mila."

Vivi was all smiles. "Hey! I've heard so much about you!"

Mila blushed a little. "Nothing awful, I hope."

"Nope, but Abby has great taste. She wouldn't hang out with anyone awful."

"Speaking of great taste," I said, "where's Asher?" I turned to Mila. "Vivi asked him to the harvest dance."

"Whoa, nice!" Mila said.

"He's getting us some food," Vivi said. "We've been dancing for a while." She cocked an eyebrow, nudging me with her elbow. "You should try it."

"We're drinking hot chocolate," I protested. Dancing with Mila sounded kind of terrifying. What if I stepped on her toes?!

"I'll hold 'em!" Vivi reached out, plucking my cup from my hands. "You have two sips left, anyway."

"Vivi!" I hissed. But she pretended not to hear me and took Mila's cup.

"Have fun!" Vivi said, grinning. She caught my eye and winked.

Oh, Vivienne Mills was *so* dead.

I wiped my sweaty palms on my pants and weaved around other people dancing to find some free space on the floor.

"Just warning you that I'm a terrible dancer," Mila said, swaying to the music.

"Oh yeah." I nodded. "I can see that. Not! This is like ring toss 2.0."

Mila shook her head, red hair flying. "No way!"

I giggled as I shook out my arms and tried not to look like I was doing some weird robot dance.

But after a few minutes, I'd forgotten to worry about whether I looked silly. Instead, I lost myself in the music and vibed with Mila. She was the cutest girl on the dance floor by far. And she was with me.

I don't know how many songs had passed, but after a while of dancing and laughing and chatting, we were both out of breath.

"Want to take a break?" I asked.

"Yes, please," Mila said. "We could grab a snack." She grinned. "I saw cheese and crackers."

"Say no more."

We walked side by side, and my fingers brushed against hers. And before I could apologize for touching her hand, she slid hers into mine. Her hand, warm in mine. Our fingers intertwined.

Ohmygodohmygod!

As we walked, I tried not to hyperventilate with worry that I was holding her hand too firmly or too softly or if my palm was sweaty or too dry. I sneaked a glance at Mila and found her looking at me.

We smiled at each other, and I tried not to stare at her glossy lips, finally ducking my head as a furious, fiery blush spread across my cheeks.

As we crossed the dance floor, heading toward the drinks and food, I didn't want this night to end.

Ever.

Focus . . . or Else

SATURDAY FLEW BY IN A DAY FULL OF homework and chilling with my friends. And by Sunday morning, I still found myself staring into space and replaying the harvest dance over and over in my mind. It had been one of the best nights of my entire life, and I couldn't wait to hang out with Mila again. Hang out with her and hopefully hold her hand again.

I still felt all floaty whenever I thought about that! Her hand in mine. We'd held hands until we'd needed them to grab plates for cheese and crackers. After snacks, the dance had started to wind down, and I'd seen Mila off to her Uber, which she'd managed to talk her parents into letting her take to and from the dance. She'd texted me a hi! yesterday and had thanked me for a great night. I'd read and reread our texts only a zillion times.

I grabbed a bus to the stable for the cross-country trial. It was a big day—riders from lots of other area stables were here to compete and test their skills.

Once I got to Foxbury, I decided to walk the course before I went to visit Beau. I wanted to have a little extra time to visualize what we'd be doing and think about it. The weather, however, had decided not to cooperate today, and it was damp and chilly, with gray clouds hanging overhead. They felt low enough to touch.

I pulled up the course map on my phone and headed to the start box. A few other riders walked the course ahead of me, counting strides and pointing out different aspects of the course to each other. Walking the cross-country course was one of my favorite parts of showing. It was quiet time that I had to myself, and I could take as long as I wanted to map out the best possible ride for Beau and me.

I took my time, counting and making mental notes about where I would have to be on extra alert with Beau. There was a tire obstacle, and it had giant bouquets of tall, twisty branches spray-painted orange for fall. The bouquets had polka-dotted ribbons tied around their centers, and they waved gently in the breeze. I knew Beau would be a little shy around the flapping ribbons and the gnarled branches.

I stopped by a stone wall, checking the time on my phone and making sure I'd been planning my speed right. So far, so good.

"Okay, so I'm going to ease him up here," I said aloud. "Then we'll tackle that bank."

It played out in front of me as I imagined urging Beau up the bank at a canter, a smile on my face because of how well we'd been doing.

"There you are! I was looking for you."

I groaned, not wanting to turn toward the oh-so-familiar voice. But I forced myself to and glared at Nina.

"Why? What else could you possibly have to say to me right now?" I asked.

"Sheesh, don't be so touchy," she said, folding her arms across her chest.

"Right. Why would I be short with you? I can't think of a single reason."

"You better drop the attitude," Nina said.

I rolled my eyes, forcing myself to stand my ground and not dart away from her. The last thing I wanted to do was stand here and take it, but I wasn't going to run away either.

"Or what?" I asked. "Oh, right, you'll tell Selly and Rebecca what I did. But did you think that through?"

"Yeah?" Instead of a statement, it came out as a question.

"If you tell them, I'm taking you down too. And then you'll have nothing over me. What I did was an accident. What you did to me? On purpose."

I smirked, knowing I was right. The more I'd thought about it, the more I'd realized that what I'd done was bad, but what Nina had done was so much worse. Rebecca would know that too if she ever found out.

"Where's your proof?" Nina asked. Now she was the one smirking.

"I have pictures of my whiteboard, emails, and texts from you," I said. "I've got all the proof, Nina."

"None of it has my name attached. You'll still have to prove I did it."

I opened and closed my mouth. She was right. Maybe? Surely Rebecca and everyone else would take my word over

Nina's if she chose to deny it. Still, I didn't want it to come down to that. I needed to focus on the show and then figure out what to do so I could still keep my secret and get Nina to stop blackmailing me.

Then a wave of anxiety hit. Everyone—Rebecca included—had known Nina longer than they'd known me. What if they took her word over mine and pointed the finger at me? In an instant, losing everything and everyone flashed in front of me. But I reminded myself that I'd never caused any trouble.

"Fine," I snapped. "Right now, all I want to do is focus on this course walk. Did you actually want something, or are you just here to poke at me?"

"I don't want anything." She raised an eyebrow. "Right now. But if I think of something, I'll let you know. Enjoy your walk!"

I gritted my teeth, saying nothing as she tossed me a casual wave and headed off to check the rest of the course.

Sighing, I stayed right where I was to give her time to get ahead of me. This was ridiculous. All of it. I'd been so wrong about Nina. Until this mess had happened, I'd been so sure Selly was the truly horrible one between the two of them. Sure,

Nina could be snarky, but most of the hate directed at me came from Selly. Or it used to, anyway.

But I didn't even have time to think about them anymore. I had to focus on what I'd done and how I was going to fix it. I'd messed up so bad by not going to Rebecca when I'd gotten Selly in trouble. And I'd made it even worse by not telling Thea and Vivi the truth. The longer I let it go, the worse it got. But I felt frozen from fear.

I started toward the next jump, almost forgetting to count strides since I was so lost in thought. Maybe tonight I could tell them. If I apologized and told them how wrong I'd been, maybe they wouldn't be furious. Or they'd be mad at me for keeping this huge secret despite them being my closest friends.

Anxiety gnawed at my stomach. *Okay, Abby, seriously. Focus on the course.* I had to or my ride was going to be a bust.

One, two, three . . . I went back to counting strides. The wind picked up, blowing a cool breeze over me. Last year, it had rained for two days before cross-country once, and it had made everything into a mud pit. Beau and I had finished the slippery course with mud caked all over his legs, belly, and chest. I hadn't come away much cleaner.

I walked down to the water section of the course, grimacing a little. There was a super-shallow lake that we had to ride through the edge of and then up a slight bank to the next obstacle. The water wouldn't even come up to Beau's knees, but I knew he was going to be anxious about going through the water. I'd have to use every trick I knew to keep him moving forward and prevent him from refusing to cross the lake.

Up on the bank, I surveyed the rest of the course. It wasn't going to be easy, especially with the water element. But I'd been doing what I could to desensitize Beau to water. Still, I knew I needed to work with him more. I had to make it more of a priority. It was hard, though, with regular riding practice and school to find the extra time. But I would have to if I wanted to work on resolving the issue.

As I walked toward the next obstacle, I crossed my fingers and hoped Beau would get through the lake without dumping me. The last thing I wanted was to go swimming on competition day, even if it would surely delight Emery, Selly, and Nina.

I tried to push it out of my head and focus on the course.

17

Selly'd

MY STOMACH TIGHTENED AS I ENTERED
the barn, looking around for Emery or Selly.
But I didn't see either of them. I was sure that
wouldn't last, though. We were all here for the competition,
so the odds of us running into one another were high.

Finally, I reached Beau's stall, let myself in, and closed the
door behind me.

"Hi, hi," I said as I wrapped my arms around his neck.
"How was your night?"

Beau leaned into my hug for half a second before jerking

his head up and snorting. I side-eyed him as I clipped a lead rope to his halter. "What's up, bud?" I asked. Usually, he was half-asleep when I came to greet him in the early morning.

But instead, he shook his head, sending his mane flying. I patted his neck and then led him out of his stall and toward the nearest pair of crossties. He crab-stepped down the aisle, looking with wide eyes at every tack trunk, as if there were a monster inside about to jump out and attack him.

Before I grabbed his grooming kit, I went over near his shoulder, whispering to him as I rubbed his neck.

"It's okay, boy. Today's a cross-country day! Our favorite. I bet that will help get you in a better mood."

Beau wasn't in a bad mood, exactly, but he was a little high-strung. Still, we had time before our round, so I could get him relaxed, and we would be ready to take on the cross-country course. I'd gotten here a little earlier than necessary too, which worked out since I could spend some time helping Beau chill.

"Hmm," I said. "I have an idea! How about a little massage?" I patted Beau's cheek.

Maybe Beau was feeding off my nervous energy. Frowning, I stepped away from him and took a deep breath. *Today's going to be fine,* I told myself. *Stay as far away as you can from anyone stressing you out.* I needed to get a handle on my anxiety today, or I was going to make Beau's mood worse. He could read me so well. Today was not the day for either of us to be nervous, not when we needed to be brave for cross-country.

I stepped back over to Beau, determined to help both of us settle down. I'd read about massages in plenty of equine handbooks and liked to give them to Beau from time to time. Standing close to his head, I put two fingers under his left eye and rubbed in small, gentle circles. He blinked a wary eye at me, but I kept rubbing. Then I switched to the other side and did the same movement.

I moved on down to Beau's neck, putting my palm on top of a muscle and pushing gently but firmly. He lowered his head a bit, standing perfectly still as I worked my way over his neck and then to his back.

While I worked, I talked to him in a quiet voice, giving him the lowdown on the cross-country course.

"So," I said, "there's one part that I'm worried about. But I want to talk you through it now, so listen up!"

Beau flicked a black-tipped ear back to me. That made me

smile. He was starting to relax now and was much more like his old self. *Whew.*

"There's a water element to this cross-country course," I explained, using a gliding technique over his back muscles. "I know the water's not your favorite. And because it's not *your* favorite, it's also not mine. But. Think of it like a giant puddle that we have to go right through the middle of to get to the other side."

Beau snorted.

"I know! But it's super shallow. It'll take you no time at all to get through it. Then we'll be onto the next jump, and you won't have any time to be grumpy about the water. Okay?"

I smoothed my hands along his back, easing up on the pressure as my hands went over his spine.

"Trying to talk him into not dumping you in the water?"

I stiffened, turning away from Beau to face Selly. She had an amused grin on her face as she sipped an iced coffee. Not a hair was out of place, and her paddock boots gleamed as if they'd never seen a speck of dirt.

"He's not going to dump me."

"Oh, so I'm imagining it that he's done that before?"

I folded my arms. "We're working through it."

"Better work through it fast. If he dumps you on the course . . ." Selly shook her head.

"I know how the rules work," I snapped.

"Of course you do." Her tone was so patronizing, it made my skin itch.

"I really can't talk right now. I'm trying to get ready for my ride."

"Good luck!" Selly winked at me. "Keep trying. Maybe one day, you'll succeed."

I bit my tongue, fighting the urge to snap back at her. But I knew better. Rebecca had a zero-tolerance policy for any kind of nonsense at the stable, but she especially didn't tolerate it during shows. I'd already taken a risk by confronting Nina, and I didn't want to push my luck and have Rebecca overhear me arguing with Selly.

Selly turned, headed back down the aisle, and I blew out a breath, hoping she'd stay away from us.

"Sorry, boy," I said to Beau. "She's always rude. But let's finish your massage and focus, okay?"

Beau eyed me, bobbing his head a little.

As I ran my hands down his hindquarters, I couldn't help but be relieved that he'd chilled a bit since earlier. I was jittery enough with everything going on, and I needed to lean on Beau. Perhaps now more than ever.

After I'd finished his massage, it was time to get Beau groomed and tacked up. The barn was teeming with riders, as everyone was in a rush to get ready for their round. I didn't see Mila anywhere, though, so maybe she hadn't come today. Hoofbeats clattered down the aisle toward me, and I looked up to see Thea, with Chaos in tow.

"Want to go groom them together?" she asked. "Away from the madness?"

"Yes, please!" I said gratefully.

I gathered Beau's grooming kit, and we headed out of the barn and to a pair of tie rings out back.

"I already got Selly'd," I said, grabbing Beau's hoof pick.

"Noooo! I tried to find you as fast as I could, but I ran into Rebecca, and she wanted to make sure our team was good to go."

"It's not your fault. She overheard me talking to Beau and made sure to tell me just how worried I was about him bucking me off and tossing me in the water."

Thea grimaced, peering around Chaos to look at me. "You didn't buy into her reverse psychology, right?"

"No way." I tilted my head. "No. I don't think. Hopefully not."

Thea pointed Chaos's hoof pick at me. "Don't listen to Selly. Ever. But especially not about that. She's trying to get in your head to psych you out. She must not think she can win on her own, so she's going to use whatever she's got in her arsenal to try and take you down."

"Shady, shady. I get that she wants to win. Hello, so do I! But I don't want to ever win like that. Not by making someone else feel bad about their riding or trying to make them anxious. We have enough to worry about when we're out there."

I ran my hand down Beau's leg and squeezed, asking him to pick up his hoof.

"Exactly," Thea said. "It wouldn't make me feel good to win like that. What's she gonna do? Gloat if you fall in the water?"

"Yes?!"

"Ugh, you're definitely right."

I used the hoof pick to gently scrape dirt and muck from Beau's hoof, taking special care to clean around his frog and along the rim of his shoe.

"Whatever," I muttered. "If that's how she wants to waste

her energy, she can go for it. I've finally got Beau calm after he was high-strung earlier, and I'm focused. I'm not going to let her take that away from me."

"There you go," Thea said. "You've got this!"

And as I groomed Beau, I repeated what Thea said over and over, trying to drown out Selly's biting words.

XC Time

WHEN IT WAS MY TURN TO HIT THE cross-country course, I was *so* ready. Before Beau and I entered the start box, I double-checked that the straps on my protective vest were tight, then checked my helmet's chin strap. Nerves made my stomach churn a little, and I tried to take a deep breath to calm myself down. But it was more of a shaky breath.

Relax, I told myself. *You're more than ready for this.*

I rode Beau into the start box, and we waited for our starting bell. Beau was quiet beneath me, both of his ears pricked forward, waiting for me to tell him it was time to leave the tiny enclosure and start on the course. While we waited, I patted his shoulder, grateful for how well he behaved and glad he'd calmed down so much.

I'd seen too many horses explode from the box, and their riders couldn't get them back under control before reaching the first obstacle. Or the horse would misbehave in the start box every time they had to enter it, in anticipation of being let out at a wild pace. That wasn't going to happen with Beau.

Good manners were important to Rebecca, and that mindset had rubbed off on me too, especially after watching Sasha Silver and her first horse, Charm, compete for years before he'd been retired. I'd seen every livestream I could of the two of them and had spent hours every night this past summer rewatching their old comps on YouTube. The chestnut gelding had perfect manners, and it was something I'd watched Sasha instill in her current horse, a gorgeous gray gelding named Sterling Silver.

The bell sounded, and I squeezed my legs against Beau's sides.

You can do this, I told myself. *Trust yourself, and trust Beau.*

I wanted a ride that would make everyone proud. A round that would make Selly seethe with jealousy. She'd already gone and had a clear ride, so I knew exactly what I had to do. It didn't have to be pretty, but it did have to be free of faults, and if we wanted a shot at a ribbon, we needed zero faults and a good time.

But maybe, even more than I wanted to beat Selly and Nina, I wanted to beat Emery. She needed to see that I wasn't going to be derailed by what she'd done to me. That she could lie, keep a huge secret, and protect the person who was actively trying to ruin my life, but I was going to get through it. I wanted her to know that no matter what, I wasn't backing down.

I let Beau into a slow trot as we left the box behind, and only when we were several strides from it did I ask him to canter.

We had our mission: no time faults, no refusals, no falls, and no runouts, which meant going around the obstacle instead of over it.

We cantered straight for the log jump, and I kept Beau's pace even and steady. He snorted, stretching his neck and back a bit, asking for a little more rein. I gave it to him but kept him firmly in check. We had a long way to go, and I didn't want him tired yet.

Beau came up to the log, and at just the right moment, I lifted out of the saddle, sliding my hands forward along his neck. He sailed over the log with ease, snorting when he landed and tossing his head.

"Good one, boy!" I told him.

As we cantered away from the log jump, I kept up good contact with my seat and hands. I wanted Beau to know I was in the driver's seat, especially before the second obstacle—the tires with the twisty branches. With the slight breeze today, I needed Beau to keep moving and not stop and be spooked by the flapping ribbons.

We cantered up toward the jump, and as it came into closer view, Beau lifted his head. He eyed the obstacle, and I felt him watching as the colorful ribbons whipped around in the breeze.

I squeezed my legs tighter and clucked to Beau, trying to keep him in a straight line without wavering. It took every trick I knew to keep him moving forward and not slow. He didn't need any time to think about refusing or running out!

My breath caught a little as we reached the jump, but Beau stayed lined up, and when we reached the tires, he was dead center. We lifted into the air, sailing over the tires, and the spray-painted orange branches whizzed by on either side of my head.

But Beau didn't wobble. He landed on the other side, and we cantered away from the tires and branches, heading for the next jump.

I let out my reins, giving Beau some room to stretch his neck as he flew over the grass with ground-eating strides. This was *so* much fun!

We lined up for the third jump, and I pointed Beau right at it. It was a fence made out of white boards with small flower baskets placed along the top. Orange and yellow mums filled the baskets, and they provided a bit of eye-popping color to the obstacle.

In my head, I counted us down.

Four.

Three.

Two.

One.

Now!

On *now*, I lifted out of the saddle, urging Beau with my legs and hands. The rush of jumping never got old. I felt weightless as I soared through the air with my horse. Beau was light in my hands as he arched over the fence, clearing the flower baskets with room to spare.

We landed cleanly on the other side.

"Nice job!" I told Beau.

I liked verbally praising him on occasion while doing cross-country.

We're doing it! I told myself. *We're having a great round!* But I tried not to get too excited. Not yet. Not when we still had so much course left. For a second, I flashed to Emery and her mare, Bliss, imagining them on the course and wondering how they would be doing at this exact point when it was their turn.

Emery was good. Really good. Unless something unexpected happened, I doubted she and Bliss would have any trouble. Not yet, anyway, since the course hadn't been too difficult so far.

We started up a slight hill, making a long, gradual turn. Beau's ears pointed forward, and there was almost a bounce in his step—he was proud of how well he'd done so far. As he should be! But I knew what was coming, and it made my stomach flip over.

Beau hadn't seen it yet, but the shallow lake was next. I needed all the good energy that we'd get through it without him making me go for a swim.

Careless

I KEPT HIS CANTER STEADY AS WE HEADED
for the lake, trying to keep my nerves in check. The last
thing I wanted was a repeat of this morning, when Beau
was anxious and feeding off my mood.

You can get him through the water, I told myself. *He's done
it before.*

Beau cantered around a bend, and the lake came into
focus, with the shallowest part marked for us to ride through.
There were a few riders scattered along the course to watch,
but I squinted, seeing two very familiar faces.

Selly and Nina.

They stood back behind the marker that designated a spectator watch spot. Nina's arms were folded across her chest, and she grinned when she saw Beau and me.

Great. Just great. They were here to see if I ended up taking a spill into the lake.

Think about the course, I told myself. *Forget them!*

I tore my gaze away from Selly, trying to focus on Beau. But my eyes shifted over to the other side of the lake, and standing off by herself was Emery. She was in an oversized Foxbury sweatshirt, almost as if she were hiding inside it. Why was she here? Did she need to come to watch me at the point in the course where I was most anxious?

Beneath me, Beau began to slow. Rapidly. He knew I'd stopped paying attention, and he was taking advantage of it. I didn't want to ride through the lake any more than he did, but we had to get through it.

I squeezed my legs against his sides, giving him a firm tap with my heels.

C'mon, c'mon, I thought.

We couldn't mess up now.

Not with Nina, Selly, and Emery right here.

Watching and waiting and hoping for us to fail.

Beau wavered and started to try and turn away from the lake. I held firm, urging him forward with my hands and seat.

"C'mon!" I said aloud. Then I clucked at him, pushing him forward. He shuddered beneath me, as if trying to dislodge a fly from his coat. Both of his ears went back, and I felt annoyance ripple through him, and I had to work hard to keep him moving forward.

We hit the water at a slow canter, and water splashed up all around us.

I kept clucking to Beau, encouraging him so we'd get to the other side, but he slowed.

Sweat dripped down my back, and I barely took a breath as we bounded through the rest of the water.

We cantered past Selly, Nina, and Emery, but I was too focused on Beau to care. It took everything in me to keep him moving forward.

A few more strides and we hit dry land. Beau snorted, throwing his head a bit as I let him slow to a trot, and we made our way up the bank and away from the water.

We did it! Beau did it!

"Yay, bud!" I cheered.

Beau's ears flicked back as he listened to me. He was going to get the biggest hug when we were done. And so many treats later!

I wanted to dance in the saddle. Or turn around and stick out my tongue at Nina, Selly, and Emery. But we had four more jumps left, and there was no time to waste thinking about those three. I hoped they enjoyed seeing us sparkle, because that was exactly what we'd done.

Beau shifted from a trot to a canter as we moved toward jump number four. I rocked in the saddle, truly enjoying myself and the ride. We'd made it over the hardest part of the course.

We approached the jump, and I let Beau out a notch. He moved easily, showing no signs of being tired, and at the right second, he rocked back on his haunches and launched himself over the pile of logs, which looked like a stack of firewood.

Beau landed on the other side, and I urged him forward. His hooves pounded the grass in an easy rhythm, and I had to be careful not to lose myself in the musical sound. I lined him up with the fifth obstacle—a faux stone wall—and pointed him toward the center. He hopped it with ease, and together, we made our way toward the final two jumps.

The first was a narrow log with dried cornstalks on either side. There wasn't much room at either end, so the cornstalks could make Beau feel a bit claustrophobic.

We cantered toward the log, and I sat deep in the saddle, ready to drive Beau forward if necessary. But he didn't even attempt to slow or shy away from the jump. He snapped his forelegs under him as his body arched over the logs.

One more! Then we'd be done!

Keep it together, Abby, I told myself. *Stay focused.*

I gave Beau more rein, letting him out a hair as we made a gradual turn toward the final obstacle—a brush fence.

Beau snorted, tugging on the reins a little, asking for more. I laughed to myself, smiling as I gave him what he wanted.

Here we go, I thought. *Last one!*

I counted down in my head, and on *now*, I lifted out of the saddle and gave Beau rein to soar.

And he did. We did. Right over the final fence, landing cleanly on the other side. We cantered toward the finish, and a triumphant grin spread across my face as I hit stop on my watch.

Take *that*, everyone!

I slowed Beau to a trot and glanced at my watch to check our time.

The numbers staring back at me didn't make sense.

We'd gone three seconds over the max time.

What? How?

I double-checked my watch again, sure I'd messed up the numbers somehow. But no. We were three seconds over and had accrued time faults.

"Uggh," I groaned aloud.

If I'd been paying better attention to our time and not worrying about Selly, Nina, and Emery, we would have come through without time faults. Beau had felt great! He'd even asked for more, and I'd held him back.

I slowed Beau to a walk and leaned down and patted his neck.

"You were fantastic, boy," I said. "I'm so proud of you."

The time faults were on me. Beau had done better than I ever could have hoped for, and I was the one who had made a careless mistake.

"I'm sorry," I told him, patting his neck again as we headed for the vet box. "I messed up."

Annoyance and anger flared in my chest. I knew it was my fault, but I still couldn't help but wonder what would have happened if those three hadn't been on the course watching me. It just wasn't fair! Why did they have to be there to mess me up?

Now, the last thing I wanted to do was see their faces. Taking a deep breath, I tried to convince myself to calm down as adrenaline coursed through me. But all I could feel was anger that the perfect ride had just slipped through my fingers.

Snapped

A COUPLE OF HOURS LATER, EVERYONE on our team had ridden. I pulled up the current standings on my phone and shook my head as I glanced at it from my folding chair outside Beau's stall.

Nina was in the lead.

Then Selly.

I was in fifth.

Emery sat further down. She'd had a refusal somewhere on the course, so I was safely very ahead of her with 1.2 penalties to her 23, with time and refusal penalties. But the more I stared at my phone, the angrier I got at seeing the name atop the list.

Nina.

The Truth X. Poser.

The person who had tried to take everything away from me and wreck my life was currently number one. Over Selly! Which, okay, that was enough of an eyebrow-raiser of its own, because Selly was usually the better rider between the two of them.

There were only two riders left, and if they didn't go clear and fast, Nina would clinch the victory. If they both did super, super well and beat her? The worst Nina could do was third place.

If Nina had simply ridden better than me and hadn't been trying to ruin my life, I would have accepted it. This was a competitive sport, and I knew I couldn't always win even if I desperately wanted to. But Nina in first place now was almost too hard to stomach. It was as if she were being rewarded for her bad behavior with a ticket to the top.

I shifted in my chair, trying to get comfortable. I'd wanted to chill with Beau a bit. Sitting here was supposed to be relaxing, but instead, I'd spent the time fuming about how my ride had gone.

Anyone is allowed to watch whatever part of the course they want, I reminded myself for the hundredth time. But it was a little different when the people watching stood there hoping to see the rider fall.

"I'm sorry, boy," I said to Beau. He'd popped his head over the stall door to see what I was up to out here.

I stood, leaving my phone on my chair, and let myself into his stall.

"Forgive me?" I asked him, wrapping my arms around his neck. "I know I messed up, but I'm so, so proud of you. You handled that lake like a pro. More than a pro! Like a horse who loves getting in the water." I squeezed him for another second before letting him go. "I knew you could do it. And I know we have lots more work to do, but I'm so happy with you."

Sure, today could have been a fluke and the next time we had to go through a body of water, Beau might react shyly and not want to go in. But today was a victory—a big one—and we hadn't given Nina, Selly, and Emery what they'd wanted. That felt great.

"I bet you sleep super well tonight," I told him. "You earned it. Now, we've got some downtime before our next one. Not much, but some." I played with a chunk of his mane,

twirling it with my pointer finger. "We're going to keep working with you around water. And jump. And do dressage. Oh,
and do conditioning with Thea. She said Chaos could use it
too, and you love him, so it'll mean more time together. But
for now, it's rest time."

I finger-combed his mane until it was neat and flat along
his neck. How he'd managed to mess it up in the short time
since I'd groomed him would forever remain a mystery.

I peered around Beau's stall, making sure everything was
tidy before I left him for a bit. He had plenty of fresh water
and a couple of flakes of hay, and his stall was clean.

I tossed Beau a smile before leaving and heading to the
main stable yard. It was packed with riders who had finished—
many of whom had their horses tied to their trailers as they
groomed them and wrapped their legs, preparing them for the
ride home.

Coaches and instructors were scattered across the yard too,
no doubt discussing their students' rides. There was nothing
to do but wait now for the remaining riders to complete their
round. Then everything would be tabulated and final placements would go up.

Overhead, dark, thick clouds rolled in, and it looked

as though the sky could open up at any second and unleash buckets of rain. For a moment, I contemplated going back to the cross-country course to watch the last couple riders, but I decided to call it a day.

I glanced around for Thea, but I didn't see her. She was probably talking to Rebecca and giving her a status update on our team.

Turning back toward the stable, I decided to go look for Thea while I waited for the final scores to go live.

"Abby!"

Nooo. I gritted my teeth, wondering if I could pretend I didn't hear Nina calling for me.

But I forced myself to turn around and look back at her as she hurried across the yard to me.

"Nina, I am not in the freaking mood right now for your games."

I bit the inside of my cheek, trying desperately not to go off on her. But the anger and resentment I had toward Nina for everything she'd done to me had been simmering below the surface since it had all gone down.

I didn't know how to handle it.

I felt like I *couldn't* handle it.

"Well, you better get in the mood," she snipped. "You're being incredibly rude to me."

"What do you want from me? Do you expect me to be all rainbows and sunshine right now?"

Slowly, she smiled. "I expect you to be polite to me. And why wouldn't you be happy?"

"Really?"

She tilted her head. "Oh. Wait. Gosh, that's right." She shook her head, frowning. "I saw the scores. I'm in first. But I didn't see your name on that list . . . did I not look down far enough?"

Rage. White-hot rage burned in my veins. I started to turn away from her, desperate to get away before I said something I'd regret. Or before I said something that would make her turn on me even more.

"Don't walk away, Abby. We're not done talking."

And then, something inside me *snapped*.

Perfect Storm

I CAN'T DO THIS ANYMORE!" I SCREAMED, whirling around and facing her. "I'm sick of you treating me like this! I'm not your puppet to jerk around, Nina."

"I'll do whatever I want. You really don't want to get on my bad side, Abby."

Around us, I was vaguely aware of heads popping up and people looking in our direction. But I didn't care. Not at this moment. I was too angry.

"What does that even mean? I already am! You already tried to do everything you could to mess up my life!"

"You deserve it!" Nina's cheeks flushed pink, and her eyes were glued to mine.

"IT WAS AN ACCIDENT!" I screamed those four words so loud, it made my throat hurt. "I told you five thousand times!"

"I don't care! You swept into Foxbury as the new girl last year, thinking you'd be on top in our lessons, and we'd all just let you take away one of the leader spots from us. But you couldn't do it on your own." Venom dripped from Nina's voice. "So you had to sabotage Selly. To try and help yourself and get your way."

I could not be hearing this right. She really thought that of me? That I was some spoiled princess who didn't like competition? Where was she getting this stuff?

"None of that is even remotely true," I said. "You think I'm afraid of competition? I'm a COMPETITIVE EQUESTRIAN!"

"How would I know what you try to do to your teammates?" Nina spat out.

"That's you! That's you and Selly. It's not me. It's never been me!"

"Are you so sure about that?"

"YES! You're projecting everything you and Selly do onto me. It's crap, Nina. I'm not going to stand here and let you try to wreck me more by saying all this stuff that isn't true. And aren't you the one spying on your fellow competitors?" I shook my head. "I mean, how else did you find out about what I did?"

Her cheeks flushed a darker pink. "I happened to be in the tack room when you came in. So what?"

"So you hid somewhere! Why?"

Her eyes flashed as she tossed her head. "Maybe I just didn't want to talk to you!"

"Or you were hoping to get something on me, which, let's be real, never would have happened unless I'd messed up and wrote down the wrong start time for Selly. I'm not the one trying to sabotage my teammates."

"Whatever you say. Actually, no. Scratch that. It's whatever *I* say. And do you want me to go to Rebecca right now? And Selly? I bet they're dying to know your delightful little secret."

"Will you shut up?" I screeched. "You've done enough! You showed up by the lake just hoping I'd fall. Admit it!"

"If you're that thrown off by someone watching you ride,

you've got much bigger problems than me," Nina said.

"But you weren't there to watch me. You came to psych me out and try to make me fall."

Nina laughed a little, shaking her head. "Wow, you're giving me so much power! I didn't know I had that ability."

I stepped closer to her, getting so close I could smell her fruity gum.

"No, I'm proving that you're a bad teammate. You tried to make it about me, but it's not. It's you. It's you and Selly and—"

"OH MY GOD, STOP IT!" Thea popped up beside us, putting her hands between Nina and me, pushing us away from each other. Her mouth was open as she looked from me to Nina. "What are you doing?!"

"Surprise, surprise," I said. "Nina's threatening me."

"Stop! Now!" Thea hissed. "Nina, just go. You can't fight at the stable! Walk away. *Please.*"

Nina snorted. "Make me."

"Are you five?" I yelled.

I was so, so angry. At Nina for doing this to me. At Selly for hanging out by the lake earlier, hoping to see me fall. At Emery for staying silent and not coming to me about Nina.

Boots crunched on the gravel, and Selly hurried over to us,

sliding beside Nina, her eyebrows raised. "What is going on? I could hear you all the way across the yard!"

"Yeah, Abby," Nina said, a wicked grin on her face. "What's going on? Maybe you should clue Selly in."

"About what?" Selly asked, looking at me.

Panic rose in my throat.

"Shut up right now!" Thea hissed. "Shut up. Both of you."

"But she—" I started.

Thea made a slashing motion. "Stop! Please. Can we all go somewhere else and have this talk? *Everyone* is looking."

"Fine!" I said. "But if Nina thinks she's going to keep—"

"Girls!"

A sharp voice cut me off, and I wanted to melt through the ground and right into the earth's core. I needed to be swallowed by the dirt, never to be seen again.

A red-faced Rebecca stormed over to us. "In. My. Office. *Now!*"

Everyone stared at us. Some riders, open-mouthed, stood frozen in place, no doubt having watched and listened to my entire meltdown with Nina. A few riders had their heads together, whispering. And I caught the stony glares from two of rival stable Lennox Hill's instructors. Their arms were across their chests as they shook their heads at us, mouths pressed in firm lines.

Oh no.

We were in so much trouble.

So.

Much.

Trouble.

So Busted

I KNEW BETTER THAN TO MAKE REBECCA tell me twice. We all did. I felt the blood drain from my face as I hurried toward the stable, with Thea at my side. Selly and Nina, silent, walked ahead of us. I tried not to cry, but I was sure tears would come any second.

I didn't dare glance up and look around at all the other students and their coaches watching as the four of us walked with our heads down toward the stable. Their stares were hot on my back.

What had we done?

What had *I* done?

I sucked in a sharp breath as the horror at what had happened started to hit me. Not only had the explosive argument happened at the stable, where it would have been bad enough for *everyone* to see, but it had happened during a competition. We had ripped apart the quiet and caused chaos.

We headed up to the second floor of the stable, where Rebecca's office was, and the four of us stood clustered together around the front of her desk, staring at the floor.

Rebecca walked in and closed the door behind her. I winced, knowing this wasn't going to be good.

She stood behind her desk and placed her hands on the top, taking a long, deep breath. "In all of my years as an instructor," she started, an edge in her voice, "I have never, not once, had any of my riders display such disrespectful behavior."

I swallowed.

"You four not only embarrassed yourselves in front of the entire community, but you embarrassed me. I'm mortified." She shook her head slowly. "I heard screaming, and my first thought was that someone had gotten hurt. A horse had gotten loose. Something serious had happened. Then, as I hurried over to find out what was wrong, I almost couldn't believe what I was seeing."

I lowered my head, wringing my hands together in front of me.

"Not only were riders fighting on stable grounds, but they were also screaming at each other during a horse show. And the riders belonged to me!" She huffed, shaking her head again. "They weren't someone else's riders. They were mine. Foxbury riders. And they were throwing a fit in full view of everyone."

"But Rebecca," Nina started, "it wasn't a—"

Rebecca stared Nina down. "I would highly advise you not to speak right now, Miss Wilkerson."

Nina closed her mouth, nodding.

"I don't care what the argument was about," Rebecca said, "and I don't want to hear excuses about why you were arguing. There has never been, and there will never be, any excuse for screaming matches at the stable, let alone during a horse show. You not only disrespected me, but you ruined the final few hours of the competition. For *everyone*."

My stomach started to hurt. She was right. The day had been nearly over, and everyone was awaiting their placements. It was a super-stressful time on a good day. Not one rider deserved to have their show messed up by four other riders who couldn't keep it together.

"Nerves often run high during a show," Rebecca said. "You all know this. Enough is going on during a competition without having to worry about people fighting. You all should be ashamed of yourselves. Beyond being angry, I'm incredibly disappointed."

We all murmured, "I'm sorry."

Rebecca rubbed her forehead. "I need you all to leave. Go back to school. I don't have anything else to say to you right now."

I glanced at Thea, both of us wide-eyed. This was bad. Really bad. Rebecca hadn't even told us what our punishment was going to be. Instead, she was sending us away.

Together, the four of us slunk out of her office in silence.

We left the stable and headed across the yard toward the parking lot, and as we walked, I noticed riders whispering and putting their heads together.

"Those are the girls. . . ."

"They got *busted*!"

". . . so ridiculous . . ."

Snippets of conversations reached my ears, which burned in embarrassment. We were never going to live this down. Oh my god, what was Mila going to think when she heard about this? She'd probably stay far away from me.

We waited for the bus, and Selly stared at her phone, suddenly groaning.

"What?" Thea asked.

Selly held out her phone for all of us to see.

Someone had caught the argument on video and posted it on their TikTok, tagging all of us. The comments were . . . *something*.

Wow, srsly??

Lol losers

Omg I'm so glad they don't ride at my barn!!

Their coach is gonna kick them off the team haha

"Fantastic," Thea said flatly.

"Do you think . . . ," I started, halting because I was afraid to hear the responses. "Do you think Rebecca's going to kick us off the team?"

I looked from Nina, to Selly, to Thea. They all had the same expression that I was sure I had: wide-eyed fear and worry.

"I don't know," Thea said.

Nina shook her head. "I don't know either."

Selly shrugged. "And I didn't even do anything," she grumbled. But there was no fight in her words. We were argued out, and now we were all just nervous. Even Selly wasn't in my face, saying how this was Nina's and my fault. She was silent. And that proved how serious this was.

There was no telling what Rebecca would do. I could wake up tomorrow and not be part of Foxbury anymore. If that happened? I shivered.

Without another word between us, we got on the bus and rode back to Saddlehill.

Now What?

THE BUS DROPPED US OFF AT THE
school parking lot, and Selly and Nina headed in
one direction, and Thea and I went in the other.

"Come back to my room?" I asked her.

She nodded, not saying a word. I felt so terrible for her.
She'd done nothing wrong—she'd tried to shush Nina and
me—but she was in trouble too. It was all my fault, and I
was a horrible friend. I'd have to find a way to get Rebecca
to realize that none of this was Thea's fault.

We let ourselves into Amherst House, pulled off our

boots, and headed upstairs to Vivi's and my room.

Inside, Vivi was watching a movie on her iPad, sprawled on her stomach on her bed.

"Hey!" she said. "I didn't expect to see you both so early." Her eyes darted back and forth from Thea to me. "Wait. What's wrong?"

I lowered myself into my desk chair, slowly shaking my head. "It's . . . it's bad."

Vivi sat up, pausing her movie. "What is?"

"I—" I started, trying not to cry. "I got into a fight with Nina. At the stable. Kind of in front of everyone."

"Oh no."

"Yeaaah. I was so—ugh! I was mad. She, Selly, and Emery showed up near the lake to watch me ride. Which, fine, what-ever, they can watch if they want. But they were there to see me fall in the water."

"Did you?"

"No. Beau was wonderful. We had a great round, but I lost focus on the course, and we got time faults. He did so well, and I messed it up for us."

"Hey," Vivi said gently. "It happens."

I took a deep breath, trying to calm down. But the

more I explained to Vivi what happened, the more upset I got.

"And Nina, she was in the stable yard. She started bullying me, and she just wouldn't stop. I lost it on her. Completely snapped."

"Uh-oh," Vivi said, grimacing.

"Oh, and Selly was there too. Of course, she *had* to get in the middle of our argument."

"Of course, of course," Vivi said. "When does she ever pass up an opportunity to do that?"

"It was *bad*," Thea said. "I came when I heard the screaming, and I was across the stable yard. Like, way across the stable yard."

"Thea came over and told us to be quiet," I said. "She wasn't involved in the fight at all. But of course, Rebecca showed up at that exact moment, and she sent all four of us to her office."

"Nooo," Vivi said. "Did she let you explain?"

I shook my head. "No. I didn't even get a chance to tell her that Thea hadn't done anything wrong. I will, though. Rebecca lectured us and then sent us back here. Zero time to explain what had happened." I turned to look at Thea. She sat cross-legged on my chaise lounge, looking small. "I promise. I'll get

Rebecca to listen to me, and I'll tell her that none of this was your fault."

"You don't have to," Thea said. "She's really, really mad. If you try and talk to her now, she'll get even angrier."

I groaned. "I'll wait until after she cools off. But I will get her to listen."

"So she didn't tell you all what was going to happen?" Vivi asked. "She made you leave without knowing?"

"Yup," Thea and I said at the same time.

My heart raced in my chest. "She might kick me off the team. I've never seen Rebecca like that. She was beyond angry."

"But even worse than that," Thea said, "was her disappointment. Embarrassment, too. But almost more disappointment than anything."

Vivi gave us a sad smile. "I'm sure she'll forgive you. She knows you two, and this isn't like you at all. You've never done anything like this before. She's upset right now, but when you talk to her and can explain, she'll be okay."

"Will she, though?" I asked. "We—and by 'we,' I mean Nina and I—screamed at each other in the yard. In front of everyone. We disrupted an entire horse show! I don't know what she's going to do with us, but it's not going to be great."

Thea shook her head. "No, it's not. I know we have to do something, but I don't even know what that is yet. I'm still in shock."

"I don't want to be kicked off the team!" I said.

"Don't say that," Thea said, moaning. "I don't want *either* of us kicked off the team! Abby, that would be the worst possible outcome here."

"I know, I know. She'd never kick you off. But I was the one screaming at Nina."

Thea bit her bottom lip. "She doesn't know that."

"She will."

I would do whatever I needed to do to make Rebecca see that Thea had nothing to do with this. It had been completely my fault. Okay, and Nina's fault. But not Thea's. And not Selly's.

"So now what?" Vivi asked.

Thea and I looked at each other. I could see the panic and fear on her face.

"I don't know," I said. "Now we wait, I guess."

"I don't think we should show up for lessons tomorrow," Thea said.

I nodded. "Agreed. Rebecca said she didn't want to talk to us right now, and it would probably make things way, way worse if we showed up at the stable to ride like nothing had even happened."

"Nothing from anyone about the trial results either," I said. "Although that's almost the least of my worries right now."

Thea picked up her phone, playing with her red PopSocket. "Should we check? What if our names aren't even on the list anymore?"

"Oh." I felt sucker punched. "You mean, what if she disqualified us and that's why we haven't heard?"

Thea nodded.

"Let's check."

Thea pulled up the final trial results, and we both bent our heads over her phone to check.

Cross-Country Trial: Final Placements

No.	Rider	Horse	Score (total)	Place
24	Nina Wilkerson	Adore	0	1
12	Selly Hollis	Ember	0	2
09	Leo Bauer	Orlando	.4	3
18	Thea Song	Chaos Gremlin	.8	4
06	Abigail St. Clair	Beau of Mine	1.2	5

"Oh my god, we're just behind Leo!" I said, squeezing Thea's forearm. "He's always tough competition."

Thea half smiled. "I'm glad our names are still on the results. For now, anyway. Rebecca could still have us kicked off."

"Yeah, I guess. But she probably would have done it already, right?"

"I don't know." Thea clicked off her phone. "Maybe? But still. It doesn't feel like a fourth- and fifth-place finish. We weren't there for the ribbon ceremony, and no one texted us congratulations or anything. Not that I expected them to," she added quickly. "But it's so weird. We always, always celebrate together as a team. Four of us came in the top five, but it feels like we lost."

It did feel like a loss. Worse than a loss. The three of us sat in silence, and all I could do was replay the whole fight with Nina over and over in my head.

Finally, I dragged myself into the shower, and Thea went back to her room to do the same. I felt sick to my stomach. It felt as though things would never be okay again at the stable. How was I going to convince Rebecca to let me stay? And how would she ever trust me again? I'd made the biggest mess out of everything, and I had no idea how to fix it.

Later, I headed for the dining hall with Vivi. We were meeting Thea for a quick, quiet dinner, and then I was going to bed. I needed to sleep off the mess that was this day. I wasn't that hungry, but I knew I needed food in my system after a long day at the stable.

In the dining hall, I got the ultimate comfort food—baked mac and cheese—and grabbed a small table in the back of the room. The dining hall was mostly empty, save for a few people I didn't know. Thankfully, no sign of Nina, Selly, or Emery, since I had absolutely no energy to even think about dealing with them right now.

Vivi and Thea sat across from me with their dinners, and Vivi watched as Thea and I picked at our food. The normally delicious macaroni and cheese tasted like cardboard. It sat heavy in my stomach, and I wasn't even remotely interested in finishing my small portion.

The more I looked at Thea, the worse I felt about everything. It would have been bad enough if this had only messed up my life. But I'd taken down my best friend too. I meant what I'd told Thea earlier—I would do whatever it took to get Rebecca to understand that none of this was Thea's fault.

"We need a plan," Vivi finally said. "You two need a plan. I'll help, obviously. But there has to be some kind of action."

"Rebecca doesn't want us to talk to her right now," I said. "So what are we supposed to do?"

"Email her, Abs." Vivi didn't even hesitate. "Send her an apology. Don't make excuses, because that's not what she wants to hear, clearly. But make it a thoughtful apology."

I put down my fork. "That's a really good idea, actually. Then I could also explain that Thea only came over to stop the fight."

"Exactly," Vivi said. "And you're not *directly* going against her wishes by emailing her. She said she didn't want to 'talk' right now."

Thea looked over at Vivi. "I bet you get this a lot, and don't let it go to your head, but you're really smart."

"I do hear it a lot, thank you!" Vivi grinned. "But it's for good reason, obvi."

"Obvi," I said, cracking a smile for the first time in a while.

We went back to eating, and I actually managed to get some food down. Vivi's idea was such a good one because it gave me something to do when I'd felt helpless before. Something to think about as a way to potentially fix this whole mess. Something I could try instead of sitting here in misery, waiting to hear from Rebecca.

After dinner, I curled up on my bed, laptop in front of me, and started writing the email. I still had homework to do for class tomorrow, but I'd have to do that later.

In her bed, Vivi was back to watching her movie on her iPad, earbuds in so the movie didn't distract me.

My fingers hovered over the keyboard as I tried to think of all the things I wanted to say. I froze for a moment, anxiety making my heart pound and my hands sweat. This email wasn't about saving myself. It was about saving Thea and getting her out of trouble.

With that in mind, I started typing, and I didn't stop until I finished. Then I reread what I'd written.

> Hi, Rebecca,
>
> I know you don't want to talk to us right now, but I need to apologize and tell you something important. Thea had nothing to do with the argument, and neither did Selly.

It was Nina and me. Thea only came over
to tell us to be quiet and try to get us to
stop. Please don't be mad at her. She wasn't
involved at all.

The argument was mostly my fault. I
snapped at Nina first, and I shouldn't have.
I know better than to do that at the stable,
and I especially know not to do that during
a competition. But I don't want this email to
be about me. I need to make things right with
you and Thea. Please, please don't punish
her for what I did.

—Abby

Before I could change my mind, I let the cursor hover over
the send button. Then I closed my eyes and sent it.

I did my homework, and then I went to bed early. My
sleep was restless, though, and it took me forever to fall asleep.
When I did, it was light sleep and filled with flickering images
of my fight with Nina. Trying to shake off the nightmare, I
rolled over and checked my inbox, hoping maybe Rebecca had
emailed me back. But there were zero new emails.

Calling a Meeting

THE NEXT MORNING I WAS AWAKE
long before my alarm went off. I'd barely slept,
bouncing from nightmare to nightmare before
finally waking up in a cold sweat and deciding not to go back
to sleep.

Vivi had hurried out the door before me, rushing to
get to class early, and I'd stayed behind to care for my plant
friends. My eyelids felt like sandpaper, and every movement
of mine was slow and lagging. I'd started and deleted a
dozen texts to Mila, but I didn't know what to say. I tried

to tell myself that maybe she hadn't heard anything, but that seemed impossible since it was all over social media.

"Hopefully, I didn't keep you up last night," I told my spider plant. I checked the soil, giving it some water with my mini watering can. "I kept having the worst nightmares."

There had been one thing that had leaped out at me in every single nightmare: Emery. She'd been in the background, in my peripheral vision. She didn't speak in any of them, but she stood there—watching and listening as I argued with Nina. Sometimes with Selly. But mostly with Nina. A sad look never left Emery's face.

"I know it was a nightmare and not real," I told my jade plant, touching her rubbery leaves with my fingertip. "But what if it was trying to tell me something? Like, something else about Emery?"

I sighed. It didn't matter. I wasn't speaking to Emery, and I had zero intention of changing that. I'd meant what I said: that I wanted to pretend she didn't exist. But even with that intention, I knew deep down that it wasn't going to be reality. I would see Emery at every riding lesson. If I hadn't been kicked off the team, of course.

Worry made my stomach hurt a little, though, because

I knew Rebecca would be watching me closer than ever if I was lucky enough to get back in the arena. I didn't want to give her a single reason to think I hadn't learned my lesson with Nina. I'd have to be chill around Emery—fine, I'd talk to her about riding stuff and Foxbury things. But I'd never, ever discuss anything more than that with her.

"She burned that bridge," I said, turning my bunny ears succulent so it could get sun on a different side.

I finished taking care of my plants, then pulled up Instagram. I stopped scrolling on a pic from Emery, posted late last night. It was an admittedly cute photo of Emery and Bliss. Emery had an arm around Bliss's neck, and she held up her gray ninth-place ribbon, smiling at the camera.

I scanned the caption. *Our XC trial for Foxbury! Can't wait for the next one!*

With a groan, I closed the app and shoved my phone into my pocket. There were going to be plenty of "next ones" with Emery and me.

"I've got to get to class," I told my plants. "Thank you for listening. I'll see you all later."

I gathered up my backpack, grabbed my iPad, and headed out. Still no email from Rebecca.

This was going to be the longest day ever.

E-v-e-r.

By world history, I was dragging. Already. I took my seat in Mr. Kemp's class and tried to go over my notes to prepare myself for today. A dull headache started to spread across my forehead, and I rubbed my temples.

"Abby!"

I jerked my head up, eye-to-eye with Selly. Her dark brown eyes narrowed, and she put a hand on her hip.

"What?"

"I said your name three times."

"Sorry. I was thinking."

"That's a first," she said, rolling her eyes.

"What do you want, Selly? I'm really, really not in the mood for whatever"—I paused to gesture at her with my hands—"this is. I just can't today."

She plopped into her seat, looking miserable. "Honestly? I can't either. Have you heard anything?"

I knew what she meant. "No. Not a word from Rebecca. Thea and I checked the trial results last night, though, and all our names were still up."

"I kept checking that too," she confessed. "I was worried that Rebecca would yank all of us."

"Me too." I took a breath, knowing what I needed to say to the other girl. Even if I desperately, deeply didn't want to. "I'm sorry."

Selly side-eyed me. "Go on."

"I didn't mean to get you or Thea in trouble. I know it probably doesn't mean anything, but for what it's worth, I emailed Rebecca last night." I picked up my Apple Pencil, rolling it between my fingers. "I told her you and Thea had nothing to do with it."

Selly's eyes widened. "You did?"

"I don't like you," I said. "And you don't like me. But it was the right thing to do. You weren't the one screaming with Nina. I was. You and Thea shouldn't be in trouble."

Selly nodded slowly. "Thanks. Let's hope Rebecca agrees with you. Because if she doesn't and I get in trouble because of you and Nina?"

"I know. You'll make me miserable from now until eternity."

"You got it."

Apologizing to Selly had felt better than I'd thought it would. For a second, I imagined telling her that I'd cost her the spot as team captain, but then I saw her furious face, and nope, I couldn't bring myself to do it. I was taking that secret to my grave.

I sat in silence until Thea slid into her desk near mine.

"You okay?" she asked in a whisper.

"Define 'okay.' I mean, I did just have a fairly decent conversation with Selly. I should probably mark that on my calendar so I can remember this moment forever. She did threaten me at the end, but what else is new?"

Thea laughed. "Definitely a calendar-worthy event."

Mr. Kemp walked into the room, and I leaned closer to Thea. "How are you?"

She gave me a small smile. "Eh, not great. I really hope we hear from Rebecca today. I just want to know what's going to happen. Whatever it is. If that means I'm being kicked off the team, tell me."

"You're not getting kicked off!"

I refused to even entertain that idea. It could be a possibility for me, but not for Thea.

"You checked your email recently, right?"

I nodded. "Even my spam folder, just in case. But nothing."

We stopped talking as Mr. Kemp started class, but my

mind kept whirling. I knew Rebecca would email us when she was ready. But I desperately wanted her to be ready *now*. I didn't know how much longer I could wait.

After school, I changed out of my jeans and into shorts and a T-shirt. I'd decided to go on a run. I needed something to take my mind off everything. And since I couldn't go see Beau or ride, it would have to be running.

I'd finished changing and was pulling on my purple-and-orange sneakers when Vivi let herself into our room.

"Ooh, can I come?" she asked, nodding to my sneakers.

"Absolutely."

I waited for her to change, and then together we left Amherst and walked toward one of the many running trails around campus. The trees were still full of vibrant green leaves, but soon they'd begin turning brilliant colors for fall. I couldn't wait for the stickiness in the air to vanish and be replaced with chilly breezes that hinted at the promise of my favorite season—winter.

"So, Nina sulked all through our history class," Vivi said. We picked up the pace, walking a little faster.

"Did she say anything to you?"

"She pounced on me the second I walked into the room. She started going off on me and telling me how you'd ruined the show, and there was no way she was going down for it."

"Me? I wasn't out there arguing with myself!"

Vivi rolled her eyes. "That's exactly what I told her. I said I didn't want to hear it. It wasn't my business, but from what I'd heard, she'd been behaving pretty awful."

"I'm so sorry. I hate that you have to deal with her too. It's so ridiculous that she's going to you to complain."

"It's not your fault. I can handle her." Vivi smirked. "I did ask her if she'd explained to Rebecca why you two were fighting. That shut her up really, *really* fast."

I let out a quiet breath of relief that Nina hadn't hinted to Vivi that she had something on me. "I wish I could have been there for that. That was the perfect question, though. She can't go to Rebecca without exposing herself unless she lies."

Which I wouldn't put past her. I tried not to think too much about it, though, because if I did, it made my stomach hurt. I kept trying to tell myself that I couldn't control Nina or stop her from going to Rebecca if she really wanted to. But if I could keep her happy-ish, maybe she'd continue keeping my secret.

We broke into an easy jog, the humid air making me sweat

already. There were students everywhere—people jogged and walked up and down the lanes and trails in their colorful workout clothes.

"Have you thought more about telling someone about what Nina did?" Vivi asked. "Maybe if you talked to Rebecca and explained that Nina was the Truth X. Poser and told her everything she did to you, Rebecca would go easier on you."

I sped up my pace, pretending to focus on jogging. "Maybe!" I said. "I haven't thought about that much. I don't want to make things worse."

I kept my gaze ahead on the path as sweat prickled along my hairline. Sweat that had nothing to do with the humidity. I felt like an awful human, and I was so stuck. If I told Vivi the truth now, about what Nina had on me and about what had happened with Selly, she'd know I'd been lying forever. She'd be so hurt and angry. I mean, I would be too.

Vivi hurried to catch up with me. "How much worse can things get?"

Oh, she had no idea.

"I don't know," I said, "but I'm afraid to find out."

"Sorry, Abs." Vivi glanced over at me. "I'm not trying to pressure you."

I looked over at my friend, watching her for a second as she looked at me with nothing but care in her expression.

"Don't apologize," I said. "I always want your advice! It doesn't feel pressure-y at all."

We smiled at each other, then turned down a stretch of trail and hit a shaded lane. We jogged in comfortable silence, and I tried to focus on my breathing and not on everything else.

But the list of everything that was wrong played out in front of me, blinking like neon signs.

* *Nina's blackmail*
* *Selly secret*
* *angry Rebecca*
* *lies to Thea and Vivi*
* *Emery??*

After our run, I checked my phone before hopping into the shower and almost dropped it at what I saw. It was a text from Rebecca to Selly, Nina, Thea, and me.

Tomorrow after school, come to my office.

My chat with Thea and Nina lit up.

Nina: It's good that she wants to meet, right?

Thea: I hope so

Abby: Finally, no more waiting

Thea: Agreed. I just want to know

I stared at Rebecca's text, willing her to say something more. Something to give us a hint about what was to come. But there was nothing.

Then my Foxbury group chat with Keir, Selly, Emery, Thea, and Nina got a new message.

Keir: Thea and I are calling a meeting. Meet us in one hour in the main courtyard. TY!

This wasn't going to be pretty. Or fun.

What Now?

AN HOUR LATER, I HEADED TO THE campus's main courtyard to meet up with everyone. I'd told Vivi that I'd heard from Rebecca, and she'd seemed to think it was a positive sign that Rebecca was willing to talk to us all. But I wasn't convinced.

In the courtyard, I spotted Thea and Keir sitting on one of four benches near one of the smaller fountains. I walked toward them, taking a deep breath. I'd texted Thea to ask what the meeting was about, but she hadn't texted me back.

She was deep in convo with Keir when I sat down across from them. Selly, Nina, and Emery trickled in after me. My eyes met Emery's, and I stared at her for a second before she looked away. She sat by herself on the bench farthest away from me, her eyes flitting from person to person. Nina and Selly, seated together, glared at Thea and Keir as if they'd been the ones to do something wrong.

Thea gave me a quick smile, then cleared her throat. "Thanks for coming! Keir and I met up earlier to talk about the state of our team—meaning, all of us as Foxbury riders— and we decided to call a meeting with everyone." She looked to Keir, nodding at him to go ahead.

"We're individual competitors, but we're also a team," Keir said. "Well, we're supposed to be, anyway."

I winced.

"We're in trouble," Thea said. "And it's not just about yesterday's argument. Our group has some *giant* problems."

"Listen, we knew some of you had a problem with each other," Keir said, glaring at each of us as he spoke. "But we thought you would at least *try* to pretend to be okay during a competition. And then the freaking Battle of Saddlehill happened in front of *everyone*. And not only did you make us all look bad, but Thea and I looked like we aren't actually good team captains in front of Rebecca!"

I cringed. He was right. He was *so* right.

"You can say my name," I said quietly. "It's okay."

Nina glared at me, but I shrugged. There was no need to dance in circles around it.

Thea and Keir exchanged a look.

"I guess Thea and I should have done something to help whatever was going on between you and Nina," Keir said. "But we didn't know it was that bad. Worst-case scenario? Rebecca kicks four of us off the team. And I'm sorry to be harsh, but that doesn't only affect you four. It upsets things for Emery and me too."

I hung my head. Keir was right. I wasn't going to argue with him. Not when he was speaking the truth.

"As a team, what we do affects everyone *else* on our team," Thea said. "Selly and I got pulled into this mess yesterday too, which isn't fair, and it made me mad."

My head snapped up to look at her. She'd never said that to me. Not once.

"I wasn't mad at you, exactly," Thea said quickly, looking at me. "I was mostly mad at myself. I should have asked

Rebecca for advice when I knew things were a mess."

"Wow," Nina muttered. "Way to be a good captain and rat out your teammates."

"I don't think you want to talk about being a good teammate right now," Thea snapped.

That made Nina fold her arms and sit back with a stony glare on her face.

"Tomorrow, four of us meet with Rebecca," Thea said. "I don't know what's going to happen, but if we're so lucky to be allowed to stay on the team, things have to change."

"Oh my god, you're not Rebecca," Selly said. "Stop it with the power trip."

"Selly, if you think that's what this is?" Keir pressed his lips together, shaking his head. "Then you can go to Rebecca yourself. Seriously, go ahead and tell her that you have a problem with your captains holding a meeting to try and fix our broken team. Be my guest."

Selly glowered at Keir but didn't say another word.

I hated this. I hated that we were here right now, having to have a meeting among all of us because of what Nina and I had done. It was mortifying. Beyond mortifying, honestly.

"None of us want to be here," Thea said. "Do you think

this is fun? For anyone? I'll answer my own questions: no, it's not. But I don't want to be back here again because of another problem. Or worse, trying to figure out what to do when someone is kicked off our team."

I shifted on the bench, trying not to look as uncomfortable as I felt.

Keir nodded. "We know Rebecca. If you all get to stay on the team? That was our pass. Our *only* pass. She will never, ever put up with behavior like this again. From anyone."

"You're right," I said slowly. "We humiliated her too. She has a reputation to think about, and we could have seriously damaged her image."

"Yeah. And that's not okay. You agree?" Thea asked Nina, staring at her.

"Yeah, fine," Nina said. "I don't want to do anything to hurt Rebecca."

"Agreed," Selly said.

Emery and I nodded.

"So, what now?" Keir asked. "How do we go viral for good and not for evil next time?"

"Better communication?" Emery asked. Her voice was quiet, and I had to turn to hear her better. "Sometimes, we may not want to say anything . . . about certain things . . . because we're worried what will happen if we tell the other person."

Okay, she was *so* not talking about our team now. I sat up a little straighter and looked at her.

"But maybe we can make a safe space, of sorts?" Emery continued. "Where we can talk about issues or problems we have with our teammates that we need to work out. Not, like, little issues, but big things that come up."

"A space to talk about these things would be great," Thea said, "because it cannot be at the stable." She looked at me for a second. "I messed up at the show. I gave Abby bad advice to talk to Nina about an issue they were having and get it out in the open. The stable was the wrong place for that. Especially during a comp. So, I'm sorry."

"You're the last person who should be apologizing," I said. "Please don't. I should be the one saying I'm sorry." I glanced at Keir, Selly, and Thea but kept my gaze off Emery. I couldn't bring myself to apologize to her. Not now. Not after what she'd done.

"Abby, it's okay," Thea started. "You don't—"

"No, I do," I said. "We're all a team. What you said earlier, about how what one of us does affects the others, is true. It's so true. I let all of you down by arguing with Nina at the stable. More than that, I could have ruined the rest of the day for every single rider there." I swallowed hard. "It was really selfish of me. It won't ever happen again. Ever. You have my word. I'm sorry."

"Thank you," Keir said.

"Thanks, Abs." Thea smiled at me.

Selly sighed, not saying a word, and I didn't look at Emery.

Thea looked over at Nina and cleared her throat.

"What?" Nina asked. "Fine, whatever, you all want an apology? A promise never to do it again? Sure. I'm sorry you were upset. I hope nothing like this ever happens again."

"That's . . . not an apology," Thea said. "At all."

"Well, that's all you're getting." Nina folded her arms across her chest. "Take it or leave it."

Thea rubbed her forehead. "This is never going to work! If you can't even attempt to be a good teammate, we're going to be right back in this same situation!"

"We're not at the stable," Nina said. "When we're there, you'll get nothing but good behavior. There. You have my word. But here? I can act however I want."

Thea and Keir looked at each other, then back at Nina.

"Fine," Keir said. "If that's the best you can do."

Nina smiled. "It is."

"I think we can go," Keir said, tipping his chin at Emery. "Let's let them talk."

With that, he and Emery got up and headed out of the courtyard.

Nina, Thea, Selly, and I looked at one another, no one wanting to speak first.

"Okay, well, if all we're going to do is stare at each other, I have things to do," Selly said.

"Same," Thea said, "but we should talk tomorrow."

"About?" Selly asked. "Rebecca's mad. We're going to get in trouble. Nina and Abby probably worse than you and me. But who knows? We might all go down." She rolled her eyes. "Yay, team!"

"I hope my email to Rebecca helps," I said. "I told her that you and Thea didn't do anything. Maybe Nina and I can offer to do something else too."

"Speak for yourself," Nina said.

"Hey, do you want to be on this team or not?" I asked.

She sighed, and a long moment passed before she finally muttered, "What are you thinking?"

"We could offer to write an apology email," I said, "to the

other stables at the show. We have all their email addresses in the directory."

"Maybe propose hosting some kind of get-together?" Thea mused. "An IPL pizza party or something. On us. Maybe that would make them hate us a little less."

"I actually like that idea," Nina said. "I bet Rebecca would too."

"Let's do it then." Thea smiled. "I think it will go a long way with Rebecca. And everyone likes pizza."

"You don't think . . . ," Selly started, hesitating, "that she's calling us in there to kick us out, do you? That would be something she could do over email, right? Like, why bring us all in?"

I chewed on the inside of my cheek. "I don't know. I really don't. But I think you and Thea will be okay. Nina and I? Not so much."

"Whatever happens, we'll figure it out," Thea said. "I'm not going to let you go down without a fight."

I shot her a smile. "Thank you."

"Are we done here with this 'Hakuna Matata' moment?" Selly asked. "We have a plan. We're going in tomorrow, and we're going to walk out as Foxbury teammates."

"Yeah." I nodded. "I think we're all set."

Selly and Nina left, heading off together.

I stayed on the bench and tried to process everything that had happened.

"Hey," Thea said softly. "It's going to be okay."

She stood and offered her hand to me.

"I hope so. I really hope so."

I slid my hand into hers and let her pull me to my feet. And side by side, we headed back across the courtyard.

"What are we doing tonight?" Thea asked. "We should do something together to keep busy."

I nodded. "I don't know about you, but I've got a mountain of homework. Want to get our stuff and meet in the library?"

"Sounds good. I'd rather cry over science homework than cry about tomorrow."

I laughed a little. "Me too."

At least by this time tomorrow, we would know our fate.

In or Out?

TUESDAY DRAGGED ON AS THE SLOWEST
day in all of history. By the time lunch rolled around,
I seriously considered claiming a stomachache and
skipping the rest of the day. The stomachache wouldn't be a lie.
My stomach had been churning since the second I'd woken up.

After school, I rushed back to my room, changed, and
grabbed the first bus to the stable. On the ride over, I pulled
out my phone and started a text to Thea, Nina, and Selly.

Abby: I'll be at the stable in a few. Going to say hi to Beau.
Want to all go in together?

Seconds later, everyone had texted back.

Thea: Definitely. Be there just a few mins behind you

Nina: Sounds good

Selly: Sure

The texts were very telling. On a normal day, if I'd ever even dared to suggest anything like that to Selly and Nina, they'd clap back with comments about how much of a baby I was and how pathetic it was that I couldn't go in by myself. But they were worried. That much had been clear all day, whenever I'd run into one of them in class.

I let my temple rest on the cool window glass, trying to distract myself by watching vehicles whiz by. Normally, I couldn't wait to get to the stable. It was my favorite place to be in the entire world. But today, I half wished the bus ride would take forever. Or maybe the bus could break down, and then whoops, no meeting with Rebecca.

But the bus didn't break down, and a few minutes later, I got off in the stable parking lot and headed for Beau's stall. I needed to see him first to give me the courage to get through this meeting. I hurried down the aisle toward where his beautiful head hung over the stall door, and he turned toward me when he heard me coming.

"Hi," I said, letting myself inside.

He nosed me, huffing softly as I hugged his neck. I let go and rubbed under his forelock, looking into his big brown eyes.

"I'm sorry I didn't get to see you yesterday. It was a long, weird day, and there's some stuff going on. But I promise—I *so* would have rather been here with you."

Beau bobbed his head a little, as if he knew my words were true.

As I looked at him, I knew I didn't want to ever, ever be in this position again. I owed it to Beau.

The only way I'd be truly free of Nina and her blackmail was if I did the one thing I'd been resisting. The one thing I'd been hiding.

I needed to tell the truth about what I'd done to Selly.

Even thinking about it still made my palms sweat and my heart race, but I knew it was what needed to happen. If I didn't do it now, I never would. And if I didn't, this entire mess with Nina would drag on forever. Or until she decided to spill my secret to Selly. Then nothing would be on my terms. I needed to be the one to do it, and this was the time.

My phone buzzed, and I looked to see a new text.

Thea: We're all here now

My knees felt a little weak, and I reached for Beau. I needed to give him one last hug.

"I'm going to do a thing," I whispered. "A scary but very necessary thing. I hope it goes okay, and that I'm back tomorrow." I dry-swallowed, trying not to let anxiety overwhelm me. "Love you. I'll see you later."

I left Beau's stall and, feet dragging, went up to the second floor and found Nina, Thea, and Selly clustered together outside Rebecca's closed office door.

"Ready?" Thea asked, her voice barely above a whisper.

I nodded.

Selly's eyes were wide, and she and Nina stood shoulder-to-shoulder, almost glued together.

Taking a deep breath, I knocked. My hand shook so hard that I almost tapped more times than needed.

"Come in," Rebecca said.

Before I could change my mind and dash away back to the safety of Beau's stall, I opened the office door and stepped inside.

Rebecca had set four chairs in front of her desk, and she nodded at them. "Take a seat, everyone."

On shaky legs, I walked over to her desk and plopped myself into the first chair, unsure that my legs would even carry me the

short distance to the other seats. Thea, Selly, and Nina took their seats, with Thea beside me. My heart pounded so loud, it almost made it difficult to hear anything else.

"Thank you all for coming," Rebecca said. "We have much to discuss."

I gulped. This did *not* sound good.

"First, I want to hear from you," she started, "since I didn't give you a chance to speak on Sunday. Does anyone have anything they want to say?"

"I do," I said, my voice high. "If that's okay."

Rebecca nodded. "The floor's yours."

I hoped my voice wouldn't shake too much. "First, before I say anything, I need to apologize. I don't know if you read it, but I emailed you on Sunday."

Rebecca nodded. "I did."

"Well, everything I said in that email was true. I'm so, so sorry about the argument with Nina. It never, *ever* should have happened at the stable. I let you down, I let the team down, and I let myself down." I took a breath as the words tumbled out. "Nina and I did not have to have that fight at the stable."

"Abby's right," Nina piped up. "It could have waited. I'm sorry, Rebecca."

"We embarrassed you in front of everyone," I continued. "Which is awful. I could have done so many things differently during the show. Like taking Nina aside in private to talk. Or going to the parking lot to talk things out. My temper just . . . took over for a minute."

"I'm sorry too," Selly said. "I didn't fight with them, but I did walk over to see what was going on. I shouldn't have. There was no reason for me to put myself in that situation."

I fought the urge to roll my eyes. Selly had come over to throw herself in the middle of our fight, on purpose, but whatever. She really hadn't done anything too wrong. Not like what Nina and I had done.

"As team captain," Thea said, "I'm responsible for everyone. I knew there was something up between Nina and Abby, but I let it go, thinking it would work itself out. I'm sorry. I should have called a meeting between the three of us and made them talk about it."

"It wasn't Thea's fault," I said. "Not even a little bit. I know she's a captain, but please don't be mad at her."

Rebecca looked at me.

"I understand wanting to protect your friend, Abby," she said. "But we are long past everyone getting off with no repercussions here. This was a serious, serious incident, and as you're all well aware, you are a team."

I shifted in my seat, seeing Thea crumble out of the corner of my eye. She was getting into trouble along with me and Nina. Selly, too. We all were sunk. I tried to ignore the nausea creeping up my throat. I felt too warm all of a sudden.

"And you will all face the repercussions for your actions as a team," Rebecca said. "I was furious on Sunday, and I've had some time to think. I'm no longer as angry as I am disappointed."

My head dropped. Hearing that from Rebecca was the worst kind of feeling.

Rebecca clasped her hands together on top of her desk. "The four of you are some of my most promising riders among all my students. And to see you arguing on Sunday? In the middle of a competition? I have much younger students who know better."

Thea sniffled beside me.

Every single second of this was awful.

"I'm sorry to say, but I haven't made up my mind about your futures here," Rebecca said.

Her words hit me like a punch to the stomach. They almost knocked the breath right out of me.

"Rebecca, please," Selly said. "This isn't fair!"

"You want to talk about fair? What was fair about four riders involved in a screaming match during a competition, Selly? How was that fair to everyone else?"

"It wasn't," Selly said quietly.

"Exactly," Rebecca said. "If you're going to whine about fairness, you can leave."

Not another peep came from Selly.

"Do you all want to be on the IPL?" Rebecca asked. "It's a serious question. The behavior you displayed indicates otherwise."

"Yes," I said solemnly. "More than anything."

"Me too," Thea said.

"Yes, I want to be on the team," Nina said.

Selly finally spoke. "And so do I."

"Tell me why you want to remain on Foxbury's team," Rebecca said, looking at each of us. "Convince me."

I swallowed hard, having a feeling that what I said— or didn't say—next could determine my future with the Interscholastic Pony League.

The Truth

MY MIND RACED. WHAT SHOULD I say? What would be a good enough reason for Rebecca to allow me to stay on the team?

I looked from Selly to Nina to Thea, watching as they mulled over the question too. They looked as scared and nervous as I was.

Then I knew what it was—what I had to say.

The truth.

"I want to stay on this team," I said, "because it's changed my life. I know that sounds cliché, but it's true. I wasn't in a great headspace when I started here. I was lonely and wondering if I'd made a mistake by going to boarding school. But this team and riding for Foxbury have helped me feel so much less alone and like I belong here." My chin wobbled. "I will show you how much I want to be here, Rebecca. I promise."

"I can't leave," Nina whispered. "I don't always show it, but this team is everything to me. I don't know what I'd do without it. I'll do better."

"So will I," Thea said. "Being named team captain was a dream come true. I didn't do a great job with it last week, but I'm going to work really hard to show you how much I want the job. Actually, Keir and I already held a team meeting yesterday, and we all talked."

Rebecca raised an eyebrow. "You did?"

"Yes." Thea nodded. "We all know we have to do better. And we, as a group, came up with an idea we'd like to run by you." Thea looked over at me.

"If you let us stay, we'd like to have the other riders who were at the show come over one day," I said. "The four of us could throw them a pizza party. We'd pay for it, obviously! But it could be our way of apologizing."

"And it would boost morale among the teams," Nina

added. "We thought it would be a good opportunity for us to show them that we're not always . . . like *that*."

"You know us," Selly said. "Rebecca, what Nina and Abby did was a blip. A onetime screwup."

I started to roll my eyes at her but knew not to so much as breathe wrong with Rebecca watching me.

"We'll all be a team from now on," Selly continued. "Let us prove it, please." She paused, looking down at her lap and then back up at Rebecca. "I know I'm not always the nicest person. But being on your team and learning from you has taught me a lot. And I'm trying to be better, which includes supporting Abby and Nina right now."

I blinked, unable to process what I was hearing. I'd expected Selly to be as rude and snarky as she was most of the time. But that was her being real and open. It wouldn't last, but it was a nice change from Normal Selly.

Rebecca sighed, running her hands through her hair. "All right. Thank you for being honest with me. It means a lot, Thea, that you held a meeting on your own and talked. I need more of that initiative in the future."

"So . . . we can stay?" I asked.

Rebecca nodded, and everyone burst into excited cheers.

But then she raised a hand. "There are conditions."

"Anything!" Thea said.

"First," Rebecca said, "and I mean this—if anything even remotely close to this ever happens again? You're off my team. I will not give second chances. In fact, consider yourselves on probation for the foreseeable future. One toe out of line, and you're done here."

I swallowed.

"Second, the pizza party is a great idea," Rebecca said, looking at me. "Nina and Abby, I want the two of you to sit down together and write the invitation email to all the other stables that participated in the show. The email needs to include a detailed apology for your actions."

My face burned. But I looked over at Nina, and we nodded at each other.

"And finally," Rebecca said, "when I said before that I have younger riders who know how to behave better around the stable, I meant it. So the four of you are going to spend some time with them. For the next few weeks, you'll be giving lessons to my beginners. You'll teach them about horse care and equine health, and walk them through the basics, like how to tack up. Got it?"

"Got it," we all said.

I wasn't sure how I would find the time to work with the newbies on top of riding and school, but I'd have to figure it out. Rebecca was letting us stay on the team, and I would do anything to keep my spot.

Rebecca's eyes landed on Thea. "I'm going to allow you to keep your position as team captain because I'm proud that you called that team meeting. That's what I need from you going forward, Thea, and I want to see you continue to take the reins with your team."

"Thank you." Thea's voice was strong. "I will."

"Good. The four of you will be spending a lot of time together with lessons and teaching, so I hope you learn how to peacefully coexist. And if you don't?" Rebecca shook her head. "Then your time on Foxbury's IPL team will come to an end."

Rebecca had left nothing unsaid. There was zero chance of misinterpretation of her words. If one of us messed up, we were out. I knew at this moment that what I was about to say could blow up my future on the team after I'd just shakily secured my spot again. But I couldn't keep it a secret any longer. Not when we needed to be a team now more than ever.

Before I could change my mind, I half raised my hand. "There's one more thing I need to say before we leave."

Secret Spilled

REBECCA NODDED. "OF COURSE."

Opening and closing my mouth, I tried to force the words out. Thea's eyes were on me, and everyone's head was turned in my direction.

"I—I made a mistake last year," I started, "and it hurt someone. I should have come forward then, but I was too scared. I knew they'd be mad at me. And I get it. I screwed things up for them. But I'm trying now, and I—"

"Abby," Rebecca interrupted. "Take a breath and slow down. What are you talking about?"

I gulped, trying to stop my heart from pounding out of my chest. My vision narrowed, and for a second, I thought I'd faint. I was too afraid to look at Selly, so I kept my eyes on Rebecca.

"Last year, Selly missed her class and got disqualified at the Beacon Hill show because of me," I said.

Someone gasped.

"Excuse me?" Rebecca asked.

"It was an accident. I erased the note on the whiteboard about the new start times because I was sure everyone had seen them, and I needed the space to ask the grooms about the feeding schedule. But then I got nervous, thinking maybe everyone hadn't seen them. So I rewrote the note. But somehow, I messed up and put the old start times. I didn't mean to!"

I felt Selly's gaze on me before I forced myself to turn my head and look at her. "I'm so, so sorry, Selly."

I half closed my eyes, waiting for her to rip me to shreds.

Instead, she burst into tears, sobbing so hard it shook her entire body.

Nina wrapped an arm around her, and Rebecca leaned forward to pat Selly's arm. It felt like an eternity passed before Selly stopped, sniffling.

"Abby, thank you for coming clean," Rebecca said. "It sounds like it was indeed an accident, but you should have come forward."

"I know," I said, miserable. "I'm sorry."

I felt Thea staring at me, but I couldn't even look in my best friend's direction.

"I lectured Selly about missing her class," Rebecca said, "and you didn't correct me."

"I should have. I was so scared to say anything. I know, it's not an excuse."

"No, it's not." Rebecca rubbed her forehead, looking at me. "Selly, I'm sorry. I came down on you when it wasn't your fault."

"Thank you," Selly said, wiping away a tear. "It was really, really painful. It was awful to have you and everyone else not believe me." She sniffled. "I was telling the truth the entire time!"

"Let me find you another tissue," Rebecca said, turning away from us to rummage in the cabinet behind her.

Selly turned and looked at me. She winked and smirked before covering her face with her hands again.

Are you kidding *me?* I'd been feeling so bad for her today and upset that I'd made her cry. But her tears weren't even real!

Rebecca found a pack of travel tissues and handed them

to Selly. She made a show of loudly blowing her nose and dabbing her eyes.

"Thank you, Rebecca," Selly said in a small voice.

"Selly, I would understand if you need to talk this out with Abby," Rebecca said slowly. "Would you like to use my office for a bit and you two can talk?"

My mouth went dry. Rebecca was going to leave me alone in a room with Selly? That was the last thing I wanted!

But Selly shook her head. "I don't need to talk to Abby about it. I can tell she's sorry."

What was *happening*?

"We're trying to move forward as a team," Selly continued, "and I want to do that. Starting now."

Rebecca smiled, shaking her head ever so slightly. "Selly, I'm very impressed. You're showing a tremendous amount of grace and maturity. This entire mess couldn't have been easy on you, and I would understand if you were angry at Abby. But this attitude? It's wonderful."

Rebecca turned to me, the smile slipping from her face. "Abby, we will be discussing this. But let's save it for another day. I think we're all talked out now, yes?"

I nodded. I was definitely at my limit for emotional

talks today, but I knew they were far from over.

"Let's leave this conversation on a good note," Rebecca said. "Thank you for coming. I'll text you with the teaching schedules, and I'll see you all tomorrow for lessons." She looked over at Selly. "Can you stay behind for a minute?"

Selly nodded, holding a crumpled-up tissue to her eye.

Heads bowed, Nina, Thea, and I left the office.

"That was . . . *brutal*," Nina said.

Thea and I nodded. I reached for Thea's arm. "Can we go somewhere and talk?"

She shrugged. "Yeah, I guess." A look flashed across her face like she really didn't want to.

"Abby?" Nina called as I started away with Thea.

I turned back around to face her.

"Why didn't you tell Rebecca?" she asked. "About what I did, I mean."

"Today was enough," I said. "One more thing, and I think Rebecca would have lost it. We caused enough trouble."

Nina took a deep breath. "Yeah, I guess we did."

"But Nina? If you ever blackmail someone else like that ever again, I'm telling her everything."

Nina straightened a bit, then nodded. "Noted."

All the fight seemed to be out of her. It was zapped from me, too.

Together, Thea and I left the stable and headed toward one of the faraway turnout pastures. The last thing I needed was for someone to overhear this convo, and I didn't want Rebecca to think we hadn't learned anything by having a serious talk inside the barn. Even though I didn't think Thea would yell. I hoped not, anyway.

We climbed the fence and settled on the top rail, looking out at the grazing horses and ponies.

"Thank you for hearing me out," I said. "You didn't have to, especially after how exhausting that talk was with Rebecca. I would have understood if you'd just wanted to talk later."

"You're my best friend, Abby. Of course I was going to listen. But I'm not going to pretend that I'm not really, really hurt."

Tears burned my eyes. "I'm so sorry. The last thing I ever wanted to do was hurt you, but I did."

"Why didn't you tell me?" Thea stared down at her lap, then looked over at me. "Did you think I would tell someone?"

"No, never! I wasn't worried for a second that you would, Thea, of course not. When it happened, I panicked. Then I felt so guilty. I messed things up for Selly, and I was so ashamed that I wasn't brave enough to come forward and tell Rebecca." I took a breath. "And I was afraid that if I told you what I'd done—and what I hadn't done—you'd look at me differently."

Thea was quiet for a long minute as she stared out at the horses, watching them graze. "I wouldn't have looked at you any other way," she said finally. "I understand why you were afraid to tell Rebecca. And not because of her! But because of Selly." She grimaced. "I get it. I promise. But if you'd told me, I would have tried to help you figure out a way to fix it."

I groaned, rubbing my forehead. "Of course you would have tried to help me. I know that. I knew it then, too, but my own anxiety got in my way. But no matter what, I shouldn't have kept something so huge from you."

"Especially when I was trying so hard to help you uncover the TXP's identity. You made it so much harder on me—and Vivi, too—because we didn't have all the facts. If I'd known about Selly, it would have made me look harder at people close to her because hello, *motive*."

"I know, and I didn't stop thinking about that for a second while you and Vivi were trying to help me. I agonized over whether I should tell you two or not, and I kept deciding not to. It kept building up into a bigger and bigger thing." I sighed. "I dug myself in deeper and made everything so much worse. I'll tell Vivi tonight, obviously, and apologize to her."

"Look," Thea started, "we all have been there—stuck and unable to see a way out. But I want you to feel like you can trust me, Abby. I'm your best friend." Her eyes met mine. "You can come to me with anything. I promise. I'm not going anywhere, no matter what your brain might try and tell you."

I choked back tears. "I'm supposed to be apologizing to you and making you feel better! Instead, you're the one comforting me." I twisted my torso, reached over, and wrapped my arms around Thea.

She hugged me back, and we both sniffled when we pulled apart.

"I do trust you. It's not you—at all." I swallowed hard. "I get scared. I don't want to lose you. Ever. And I'm afraid I'm going to do something that will make you stop speaking to me."

"Abby." Thea's voice was soft. "What happened with Selly was a mistake. You didn't do it maliciously to hurt her and ruin her life. Right?"

"Right."

"Then you had nothing to worry about with me. The only

thing that could drive us apart is if you don't tell me things and you hide them from me. That *will* drive a wedge between us."

I nodded. "You're right. I'll come to you from now on, I promise."

"No more secrets," she said.

"No more secrets. Ever."

"Okay, good." She gave me a small smile. "Want to come say good night to Chaos with me?"

"Absolutely."

Together, we climbed down from the fence and started back toward the barn, relief coursing through my body.

We were going to be okay. Thea wasn't ditching me and never speaking to me again. She was giving me another chance, and I wasn't going to mess it up. From now on, I was telling her everything. Always. No matter what.

Out for Blood

AS WE WALKED BACK TO THE STABLE, I took a deep breath, trying to shake off the anxiety that made my skin prickle.

"So, on a scale from zero to ten, how worried are you about Selly?" Thea asked.

"Oh, you know, just a solid five thousand."

Thea winced. "She's going to be out for blood."

"I know, and I'm really hoping that after everything Rebecca said, she'll leave me alone for a while."

"We can hope! Rebecca was serious about us messing up,

and the last thing Selly wants is to get kicked off the team."

Inside the stable, I peered down the main aisle, looking for Selly, but I didn't see her anywhere. Maybe she'd left Rebecca's office and had gone back to school. Or maybe she was still with Rebecca, crying about what I'd done to her.

I followed Thea down to Chaos's stall, and we let ourselves inside. The big gelding was dozing in the back, but he pricked both ears forward and nickered softly when he saw Thea.

"In Rebecca's office," I said, "you said you were mad about my fight with Nina. I know I shouldn't have kept the whole Selly thing from you, but I want you to be able to come to me too, Thea. I didn't know you were mad."

She reached for a knot in Chaos's mane, taking her time untangling it with her fingers. "I was more scared than anything, I think. Everything happened so fast, and yeah, I wasn't happy that you and Nina got into that fight during the show, but there wasn't much time for me to stay mad. We had to come up with a plan to make sure Rebecca didn't kick us off the team."

"That was all you and Keir. Calling that meeting saved us."

"The pizza party idea did too."

"Now I'm worried," Thea said, "that Selly's going to retaliate and do something to get all of us in trouble. Trouble we won't be able to come back from."

"If she's going to come after anyone, it better just be me. You didn't do anything."

"But we're a team, remember?" Thea sighed as she finger-combed Chaos's mane. "Rebecca made that clear."

I reached out to rub his nose, then let his soft whiskers tickle my palm. "I know. You're right. I don't want this to get out of control like it did with Nina."

I knew what I needed to do, even if I'd rather do *anything* else. But if I didn't, I wouldn't be doing everything I possibly could to try and smooth things over with Selly.

"I'll ask Selly to talk," I said. "I don't know if it will do any good, but I'll try. At least I'll know I attempted to handle it better than I did with Nina. We can talk at school, which is far, far away from the stable, and I'll try to get through to her that we can't make another mistake."

"That's a really good plan, Abs. As your team captain, I appreciate it. Greatly. And as your best friend? I really, really hope she listens."

"Me too."

I sneaked a glance at Thea, watching as she patted Chaos

and smoothed his forelock. Deep down, I was still worried that Thea was angrier at me than she let on. I knew I needed to give her some breathing room and let her process everything that had just happened. Maybe I could do something special for her this week, something to apologize and help make up for everything.

She and I finished saying good night to Chaos, and then I decided to go check on Beau while Thea headed for the bus.

I was glad for a few moments of quiet alone time with him after the roller-coaster day I'd had. At his stall, I peered over the door.

Beau looked up at me from his water bucket, water trickling down his chin.

"Don't let me interrupt," I said, laughing a little. "Hydration is of utmost importance!"

But Beau started over toward me as I opened his stall door and let myself inside. He shoved his wet muzzle into my arms, leaving a trail of water along my forearms.

"I wanted to tell you that I did the scary, hard thing," I whispered. "And things are still a mess, but they're better than they were before. I think? Hopefully."

Beau blinked, watching me as I talked.

"The thing that's definitely better is that all my secrets are out in the open now. And I didn't get kicked off the IPL team. So we're back to work tomorrow, boy."

I hugged Beau's neck and gave him an extra-tight squeeze before letting go.

"I'll be around a lot more over the next few weeks," I told him. "Rebecca wants us to work with the newbies. So I'll be peeking in to say hi whenever I can."

I lightly scratched Beau's shoulder with my nails, feeling wiped. Ever since the fight with Emery, I'd been on the edge. The blowup with Nina hadn't helped, obviously, and now I felt waves of anxiety even thinking about going back to school because of what I needed to do when I got there.

Talk to Vivi.

I'd have to tell her everything that had happened today and all about the giant, awful secret I'd been keeping from her. It was extra hard to tell Vivi, since she'd been the one to work out the TXP suspect list on the whiteboard with me and had painstakingly gone over each name on the list with me to try and figure out who had been my blackmailer.

Vivi will understand, I tried to tell myself. I hoped I was right, but I wasn't so sure. I wished I could stay in Beau's stall forever, honestly. A place where I could hide out and not have to go face up to what I'd done. But I owed it to Vivi, I knew that.

I told Beau good night and went up to the second floor to check the turnout schedule and make sure Beau was getting plenty of time outdoors. Everything looked right on the board, so I made my way back down the hallway, barely paying attention as I went down the stairs and—

Selly appeared out of nowhere on the landing and grabbed me by the upper arms.

"Oh my god!" I hissed. "What are you doing?"

"Shut up," Selly said, her eyes locked on mine. She held a fistful of my T-shirt in each hand, almost pinning me to the wall. "Remember, one peep and Rebecca will kick us off the team."

"Okay, okay! But you can't shove me into a wall, Selly! That's next level, even for you!"

"Then yell. Go ahead."

I gritted my teeth. I knew she was right. One hint of trouble, and we'd be off the team.

"I'm sorry," I said in a hushed voice. "I didn't mean to make you late last year. I would never—"

"Oh, save it. You're too much of a goody-goody for that kind of sabotage. But it doesn't matter. You still did it. And those tears I faked back in Rebecca's office? You're gonna be crying a river for real by the time I'm done with you."

"Selly, come on," I said. "What about what Rebecca said? If we get caught messing up, we're off the team. No more chances."

"Bingo. You said the magic words. 'If we get caught.' And I won't."

Anxiety made my chest hurt. Every word Selly had uttered in Rebecca's office about teamwork had been a lie. She was going to do exactly what I'd been worried about—make my life absolutely *miserable*. I knew how Selly was, and there was nothing I could do or say to make her give this up.

She let go of my T-shirt and patted my right cheek. Roughly. "See you tomorrow, St. Clair."

Selly left me shaking on the landing, and I knew nothing was ever going to be the same.

Acknowledgments

Thank you so much Josh Getzler for all your wisdom and support. All the thanks to Jonathan Cobb and everyone at HG Literary.

Aly Heller, we are knocking these out! As always, you're the best to work with, and I'm so lucky to have you in my corner. Jessi Smith, thank you for being delightful and helping me make Saddlehill shine.

S&S is such a great place to call home, and thank you so much to Karin Paprocki, Mike Rosamilia, Sara Berko, Kilson Roque, Valerie Garfield, Kristin Gilson, Anna Jarzab, Chel Morgan, Valerie Shea, Olivia Ritchie, Kaitlyn San Miguel, Alissa Nigro, and Nicole Russo. Lana Dudarenko, you nailed this cover, and I love it so much!

Thank you, as always, to my parents for all their support and encouragement. And to Lorrie and Speedy for welcoming me into the neighborhood with such warmth.

Shanna Alderliesten, you're always my first reader, and

thank you so much for helping me with any horsey questions.

Tess Sharpe, I'm so glad we're friends! The writing Zooms with you and the Trifecta give me so much to look forward to, and I adore every single person in our group. The wisdom, support, and friendship mean so much.

Misty Wilson, my must-always-be-writing twin, one day we will be indoor cats together where we'll have snacks, write, and rewatch JatP.

Julia Hezel, there's not a better bestie than you. I hope you know how much you mean to me.

Thank you to Jen Kurtyak for providing me with a wardrobe of cozy hoodies (heh!) and for listening to me talk endlessly about how publishing works.

Booksellers, librarians, and teachers, thank you as always for everything you do!

Finally, to my Harts, I get to do this writing thing because of you. Thank you for being the best readers a girl could ask for!